PATTERN IN
BLACK AND RED

PATTERN IN
BLACK AND RED

Faraday Keene

COACHWHIP PUBLICATIONS
Greenville, Ohio

Pattern in Black and Red, by Faraday Keene (pseud.)
© 2017 Coachwhip Publications

Title published 1934
Cora Jarrett (1877-1969)
No claims made on public domain material.

Front cover: Dagger © Nixken

CoachwhipBooks.com

ISBN 1-61646-396-1
ISBN-13 978-1-61646-396-0

ABOUT THE AUTHOR

Faraday Keene was the pseudonym of author Cora (Hardy) Jarrett, born in Norfolk, Virginia, in 1877. She was educated in Pennsylvania (Bryn Mawr College), at the Sorbonne, and at Oxford University. She married Edwin Jarrett in 1906, and they had three children. Cora Jarrett went on teach English and Greek. She wrote several well-received novels (*Night Over Fitch's Pond*, etc.) and numerous short stories. As one newspaper review noted, "Miss Jarret [*sic*] signs all of her mystery and short stories with her pen name and her authentic novels with her real name" (St. Petersburg *Times*, Nov. 30, 1934). Cora Jarrett died in 1969, in Putnam Co., New York.

FOREWORD

OUT OF RESPECT for two groups of persons of distinguished record, it is but proper, though it should be unnecessary, to say that the names, personages, geography, and incidents of this history are wholly fictitious. Avery Dunn, his relatives, his descendants, and his family seat, are apocryphal in every detail, and in no way connected with those well-known Southern families the Averys and the Dunns, whose interesting names he unworthily wears.

I am tempted to add a word about how this book came to be written.

Perhaps I should never have had a full-length mystery-story to my credit, had it not been for an experience that was somewhat surprising to me. Having published, under my own name, my first novel—a psychological and emotional drama of married life—I found to my astonishment that in certain bookstores (this was in the United States only, it did not happen in England) the book was offered for sale as a "mystery." I need hardly add that with readers devoted to this fascinating genre, of which the rules are in their way as definite as those that govern the sonnet, it had little success; it takes more than the enigmatic death of a character to make a mystery-novel.

Now, have you ever played chess? If you have, and if an onlooker has said to you, "I see you are opening with an Evans gambit," when in fact you were opening with something else, what did you do? If you are like most people, in such a case you answer, "No, the Evans gambit is so-and-so." In other words, you show him.

Pattern in Black and Red is my Evans gambit.

Faraday Keene

CHAPTER I

"You'll realize that to a man of my age the shock has been considerable. May I sit down?—And who had the opportunity to perpetrate this appalling crime, my dear Mr. Wing?"

I answered with some irony, for I needed an answer to that very question myself; we had been going over and over this same thing with the sheriff for hours. "Practically the entire population of the United States had an opportunity to perpetrate it from outside the house, since the situation was the stereotyped one: he was alone, and the windows were open. If murderers were sportsmen enough to pick a time when the victim had the windows shut, and was surrounded by other people—"

"Now, Carty!" protested my wife.

I gulped and went on. "So the field for suspicion is wide. To begin with, it includes all the servants except the butler."

"Carter, you are simply confusing the professor."

I said, "My dear, I'm confused myself. Everybody is confused. Why shouldn't the professor start even with the rest of us?" Our visitor just sat with folded hands looking at me. I continued "The list of suspected persons includes even my own harmless-looking wife, here present, who could easily have committed the murder if she had done it in collusion with her brother and Miss Avery; they were out in a car somewhere, they say they were driving about. And our invalid neighbor Dr. Moreland is known to have been out at the same time, quite alone. Also driving about.—Inside the house, the butler and your young friend Allison share a rather tricky alibi; no doubt it can be exploded. Next, there is my cousin Miss Lydia Perryman, an active old lady of seventy-six, who had a chance to murder Mr. Voorhees single-handed, though the evidence of the *rigor mortis* is against her candidacy. My other cousin, our host, Shadwell Dunn, who is more active still, being thirty or forty years younger, points out that he also could have done it, with the help of a confederate outside. In fact, Professor Ames, I myself alone under this roof—or in this part of Frisbie County, as far as we can tell—am not under suspicion. That is the state of the case."

The little old gentleman regarded me gravely and bewilderedly. "In other words, there isn't a single person who can be really suspected. You are at your wits' end, you are irritable and exhausted—you want nothing but sleep. And here I come to keep you out of your bed awhile longer. I do assure you I'm sorry."

He looked sorry, he sounded sorry. But the clock in the hall had struck the successive quarter-hours seven times before he rose to his feet and, said, "I think I am now acquainted, with the details."

This was no overstatement. I had realized, in the first five minutes, that never before had I seen a thorough-going question-asker in action. Professor Ames wanted specific information, and he got it. He now knew the plan of the house, and how the windows fastened, he knew the servants' names and ages, he knew when Cousin Lydia took her nap. I need not say that Gertrude had been doing most of the answering. Having blown off my steam, I had quite sincerely begged our visitor's pardon for being a smart-aleck, and had yielded the floor to my wife. And as her brother Freddy would say, details are Gertrude's meat.

She gave the professor almost all the data he needed for his grisly and astonishing theory of the crime in that first interview. Hardly an element of importance in the history of those thirty hours between the arrival of Matthew Voorhees and his death did she fail to recall; Ames has said as much since then himself. "Nor were there very many, my dear," he added with his mild little twinkle, for by that time he and Gertrude were friends for life, "that you failed to misconstrue!" One omission she did make: except for the episode of the vacuum cleaner, which helped to fix the chronology of the afternoon, she left out any significant mention of the colored people in the house. This slip had peculiar consequences, and was only repaired by accident fortunately before it was too late.

But as he stood now, peering at us over his glasses, when Gertrude had finished her tale, you would have said that Professor Leonidas Ames, the well-known ornithologist, was the unlikeliest person in the world to guess anything that wasn't spelled out for him. He was trying hard to look like a competent criminal investigator. His lips, in his mild old face, were compressed in what he doubtless believed to be a formidable line. His brows were drawn down. But under them his vague blue eyes looked as naively excited as a child's. He rumpled his mop of white hair vigorously.

"To a man of science," he said, "each fresh detail should be a fresh source of enlightenment. But in dealing with an unsolved crime, the reverse appears to be the case." He rumpled his hair again.

("Pretending that he couldn't see a glimmer! Picture of an ornithologist stumped. A scientist up a tree," as Gertrude says to this day. She concludes, affectionately, almost proudly, "A bland old white-haired liar!")

"Take just one thing for instance," he went on in his lucid little classroom manner. "You tell me that during the quarter-hour preceding his death Mr. Voorhees was observed to be apparently flashing a signal to someone outside in the grounds—"

"Unless we assume," I interrupted, "that the signaling was done by the murderer, either before or after the murder, to a third person. Seems brainless, but—"

"Not at all. It sounds rather horribly clever, for see how it confuses us! If we knew who was responsible for those flashes, and why, and whether it was after or before the crime, we should know the whole story." He spoke almost severely, as if he thought I should produce the information at once. "You saw no indications at all? Yet you made the first inspection."

I said consecutively no and yes to that. Gertrude added, "There was my brother Freddy, too."

"Ah, just so. I wish we had your brother here." Ames had clearly not thought much of me as a source of information since he learned that I had been deep in a book on the sofa, for the space of a full hour, before, during, and after the crime.

"Good grief!" said Freddy afterwards, when I described the professor's disappointment, "did he think you should, have been leaping about the house picking up clues and filing 'em for future use in case somebody got murdered?" Freddy is red-haired and irreverent, and his sister adores him.

Ames went on, "It is unfortunate that no scientific observer was present."

"It is even more unfortunate, my dear Professor Ames," I said, "that a whole lot of observers, scientific or otherwise, were not present in that particular room twenty minutes earlier. Say at five minutes past nine. Then there would have been no murder at all."

The professor shook his head. "I see clearly that you do not possess the research-temperament, Mr. Wing, and the habit of analyzing phenomena. I think you'll find that this particular murder was inevitable. Time and place might have varied, but the outcome would have been the same. When a human life is taken as cold-bloodedly as in this case, the motive must be strong."

He was as didactic as he was gentle, now, but he was also blinking with drowsiness, and I said to myself, "Poor old duffer, it's time to get him to bed. He'll analyze these phenomena just about as well in his sleep."

But when I said as much to Gertrude, after our bedroom door was closed, that remarkable woman only said to me reprovingly, "He's sweet, Carty. And he has more brains than you and the sheriff and Shadwell all put together."

It was a grim and—at the time—incomprehensible ordeal that I lived through in the week that was to follow, as a sort of second-in-command to my cousin, the owner of our great-grandfather's old house of Handsome Creek. On that night of Ames' arrival, alas! the ghastly business was just beginning. It lasted for seven days and nights of mounting horror and surprise. I suppose the little professor, with his mop of white hair and his quaint wool-gathering ways, is really the hero of our strange adventure. Unless the actual hero is his colored servant Robinson. Each of them would tell you it was the other.

To give any idea of that terrible week, I must first go back, and tell, as Gertrude told it to Professor Ames, the story of the two days that had just passed.

Ames' own arrival was after midnight on Tuesday night—which was really, of course, Wednesday morning. Voorhees, bringing a young friend with him, had appeared, with only telegraphic notice, on Monday afternoon. He was a former schoolmate of Shad's, but to the rest of us he was a stranger. "I believe he's a very successful corporation lawyer in New York," my cousin said. And Voorhees looked the part. Impressive and very slightly pompous, but likable and genial. At the moment he was a bit drawn and pale. From a recent operation, he said.

"But why in heck," I asked Shadwell, "does a man in that state pick this sizzling time of year for a visit to the South?"

"Can't imagine," said my cousin. "He could have taken me up on that invitation any time these last three years or so. I told you his wire was a bolt from the blue. I hadn't laid eyes on him or heard from him, since that day in Johannesburg."

It was, in fact, just a coincidence, and a four-year-old one at that, that brought Voorhees to Handsome Creek and to his so-inexplicable death. He had run into Shadwell by accident, on a trip to South Africa, just before my cousin wound up his affairs there, and came home; and recognizing an old classmate, had recalled himself to Shadwell's memory. "With some difficulty," he had ruefully confessed, and Shadwell had tactfully denied, for Voorhees looked an old man for his thirty-nine years, while my cousin looked a young one. Forty-five and thirty-five you would have called them. The difference was almost depressing, especially after you had seen their young likenesses as schoolboys in a group picture that Cousin Lydia produced from an album. In the photograph Voorhees was the healthy-looking one, with his round chubby face, and Shad was skinny and sick-looking and under-sized, with dark unhappy eyes under our high ancestral forehead. ("The one point of family resemblance," as Gertrude said to me for the hundredth time, "between Shad and you!")

The two of them, meeting after so long, had apparently found a lot to say; Voorhees was the hearty-do-you-remember kind. Moreover, he recalled that he had a sort of cousin, a Dr. Moreland, who had just settled somewhere in Frisbie County. He produced a copy of the Frisbie County *Register*, from a correspondent at home who had spied this item: "Dr. R. Moreland, Well-Known Scientist, Takes Lease of Elmington." Why, the old house called Elmington was not a mile from Handsome Creek! Shad told me the sight of the funny little county paper made him feel like a boy again; he hadn't seen a copy for years. It wasn't changed a bit. The editor was still naively bragging about the magnificent climate of Frisbie County, partly because the well-known scientist had chosen it, partly because the oldest inhabitant, just deceased in the poor-house, had lived to the ripe age of a hundred and two! Which had reminded Shadwell to mention to his old friend that he was moving back to Frisbie County very soon, for good; he had made money enough, he didn't care about being a multi-millionaire. If Voorhees was ever anywhere near Handsome Creek, he must stop for a visit, and sample the magnificent climate, and look up his kinspeople. And now here was Voorhees, four years later, dropping out of the blue!

"It's all right with me," said my cousin. "He's one of the best. And that's a nice young fellow he has with him, though I wish he wasn't so quiet. He acts as if he had something on his mind."

"Voorhees says young Allison has business in this neighborhood. Maybe that's why they came."

"He seems keen on getting in touch with his guardian, the old professor they keep talking about. But they'd hardly have come all this way just for that."

But it really was just for that, we soon learned from Voorhees, that they were there. He told us the story. He seemed very fond of Allison and very proud of him.

The boy, he said, was pluckily shouldering the deficit on a slightly shady deal he had been enticed into, in all innocence. "Some of his friends put money in, on his advice; he won't let them lose. He's laying the facts before Professor Ames, his guardian, and asking for an advance on a small estate that's coming to him when he is thirty years of age. If Ames refuses, I'm ready (and have said so) to put up the sum myself. In fact, the certified check is in my trunk this minute, ready. But it won't be needed. Professor Ames is a very fine old fellow. Eccentric, but a splendid type. He'll understand." In conclusion, he asked us to let Allison go on thinking that, except for the two of them, nobody knew.

So we were informed about the nature of Allison's errand, but he did not know that. We were to remember the fact later on,

The story increased my liking for Voorhees. And for his part, rich Yankee though he was, he appeared to have fallen in love all over again with the simple Southern ways he had known for a short time as a schoolboy. He was interested in everything about the place and the surroundings; he catechized my dear old cousin Lydia by the hour. These two people were already like old friends; they enjoyed each other extravagantly. Gertrude said, "Your great-aunt, my dear Shadwell, is embarked upon a perfect *affaire du cœur* with your boyhood friend. He has been in the house exactly one night, and already to Cousin Lydia the rest of your guests are empty shades!"

The truth was, my cousin Lydia loved a listener. And Voorhees, whittling lazily, letting the shavings drop and drop about his feet (in his nervous state, this was his favorite amusement), seemed to find endless entertainment in her discourses on the family tree ornamented by herself, to say nothing of Ann Page and me, but of which the crowning glory, to Cousin Lydia's stoutly partisan mind, was his own one-time schoolfellow Shadwell Dunn.

As my wife explained this favoritism (she loves to explain my own family to me): "It's not just that her great-nephew Shadwell is handsome and rich, or that he made his money in years of romantic wandering over the earth, or even that since he came home he has been more devoted to her than most sons are to their mothers. It's because he's such a perfect 'family piece'! So exactly the image of the ancestors he ought to look like, without a trace of the awkward ones or the stupid ones or the bow-legged ones—yes, even *your* sacred family tree, darling, bears that kind on its less distinguished twigs, here and there! Shadwell has the Dunn legs and the Avery brow, and his lower jaw comes straight down from Governor Spottswood or somebody. He's like all of their nice old portraits rolled into one—and it makes him look like the Fortunate Prince."

But nothing less like the lot of a fortunate prince could be imagined than some of the hours that were ahead of Shad. And it might almost have seemed that Voorhees struck the note of what was coming, in a certain question to Cousin Lydia.

"Do you mean to say," I heard him demand of her, in a tone of piercing reproach, "that I've had the incredible luck, for twenty-four solid hours, of staying in a house with a curse on it—an honest-to-God curse—and haven't been told?"

She nodded her gray curls brightly.

"Then," he exclaimed accusingly, "just wait till that fellow Shadwell Dunn comes back!"

We were on the deep shaded west porch, that blazing afternoon, killing time until it was late enough to go fishing. There were five of us present at the moment; the two younger men of our party had had to drive to the village, and Shad had just gone into the house. Cousin Lydia sat erect in her favorite stiff-backed chair, pleased with the impression she had made. She was small and spare and seventy-six; she had black, snapping eyes in her little wrinkled face, and the softest Southern accent that ever failed to disguise a rock-ribbed strength of mind. Gertrude and I looked on, too limp to smile; and when my wife is really limp, it is only because the weather is very trying indeed. Gertrude is as keen as she is handsome; she has sparkling green eyes—at least they sparkle in cool weather—curly red hair, and a few intriguing freckles. The fifth person on the porch, Ann Page Avery, eighteen years old, and very lovely, who has no freckles, and whose hair is a brown-satin cap on her graceful head, was at the moment fiddling through a game of solitaire. Our temporarily absent cousin had had the right idea: he had gone to summon the drinks.

Voorhees, in a deep chair with his rather short legs comfortably extended, was a picture of content. Ever since he arrived, he had been in ecstasies over his surroundings. He now confessed, "I've a passion for old furniture and old houses, and a very special passion for family mansions with an overhanging doom!"

Shadwell's old-fashioned house, Handsome Creek, so named from the fairly considerable stream that half-circled the fine hill it stood on, was an ancient dwelling, originally modest in size, but much enlarged in 1852 by Heriot Dunn, and now completely modernized by Shad. Its great length was from end to end, and by comparison its depth was shallow, not more than forty feet from front to back, as you looked through the hall. It had two fronts. In the middle of the northern one, the hall door opened on to a terrace, flush with the lawn for most of its length; to the south the ground fell steeply away, and there were broad stone steps where the drive made a circle in front of the portico, with a tall green wall of hedge around it.

Inside there was everywhere that fascinating waste of space that is the charm of old remodeled houses. The big delightful drawing-room was practically useless, except as something you walked through to get from the hall to the billiard-room. This was the largest room of all—even the billiard-table looked small at one end of it. It had many windows, a wonderful great fireplace, deep sofas and chairs, plenty of ash-trays, and not too many flowers. It was in practice our general living-room, and it filled that whole end of the house.

On the other side of the hall that cut the house in two, the waste space took the form of a wide transverse corridor that went off at right angles, forming the shank of a T, and ended at the door to the west porch—an arrangement permitting a person at the far limit of the billiard-room to enjoy, across the drawing-room and hall and down the corridor itself, an uninterrupted view from end to end of the house. This I have good cause to remember, for it was I who, just a few hours later, from my distant seat, saw Voorhees make his last ill-fated entrance by that very door.

On the corridor's north side was the long library, its windows opening on the terrace; across from it, the dining-room, with the pantry beyond. The kitchen was downstairs.

Such was the arrangement of the principal rooms at Handsome Creek. All spaciousness and charm, with gleaming floors and beautiful old mahogany and satin-wood furniture polished and rubbed to brightness, the old house drowsed behind us, lovely and tranquil, that fatal afternoon. To think of it as under a doom seemed a fantastic thought indeed.

The flourishing state of my cousin's house and farm was owed to the fortune that he had made in a far country. He had exactly reversed the story of the Prodigal. He had run away from school as a boy of seventeen, and had never come back to face his irascible father; Avery Dunn had died without seeing his son again. And while Avery Dunn and the other landowners of the district were growing poorer and poorer, Shadwell was picking up property on the other side of the world. When he reappeared in Frisbie County, some years after his father's death, and bought back Handsome Creek from the creditors, the old house blossomed forth in more than its ancient splendor; the fine furniture was restored and recovered, the floors shone with wax, the garden rose again out of a sea of weeds. Shad himself, a rather silent being, might have found himself too old, and too strange, in his middle thirties, to fit back into the old life, if he had been alone. But he did an act of kindness that turned out a wonderful stroke of policy: he sought out his father's aunt, Miss Perryman, and brought her home to live with him. And Cousin Lydia was a natural and irresistible magnet; the house filled up with cousins and aunts and uncles and family friends who came and went and came again, and brought everybody they knew. The nicest part of it," said Gertrude warmly, "is to see Shadwell get so much solid fun out of having had a kind impulse toward his great-aunt. Kind impulses don't always pay so well!"

But though Cousin Lydia was the most cheerful of women, she dearly loved the legend of the curse. Or as Freddy Gibson called it, the hex. And I blessed the happy thought that had made her mention it now. The story was the sort on which Cousin Lydia, always a fluent teller of tales, could be trusted to put forth all her remarkable powers.

It would create a diversion that was much needed. Tension was in the air that afternoon, a troublesome consciousness that certain subjects must be kept off of. And to cover up such awkwardness, what is better than a sprightly monologue, from a lady full of reminiscences?

It seemed odd that the coming of so agreeable a person as Voorhees should have involved us in conversational taboos. But so it was. And six hours later we were horribly perplexed to decide which of them had a sinister meaning, and which had not.

The first taboo was on the subject of his African travels. This he himself had brought about, by rousing the superstitions of the servants.

The negroes had been already on edge. The pantry-maid Georgia, who was the old butler's daughter and also the household problem, was having one of her periodical explosions of religious mania. Her wild looks and mutterings and midnight ramblings were harmless, but they were agitating while they lasted. And she was more hysterical than usual this time, with a childlike grief: her beloved mongrel dog had found some poisoned meat meant for his sheep-killing brethren, and eaten it. The veterinary had been working over him, quite hopelessly, all day. And just at this pitiful little crisis Voorhees had happened to bring out from his luggage, as a present for Cousin Lydia, an African fetich, an intriguingly repulsive little black figure about eight inches high, carved in wood. The mere presence of this object in the house had impressed the colored people, for some reason, as calamitous. Old Isham, the butler, had actually refused to look at it; at least, when invited to do so, he had merely run his fingers over it, with averted eyes, and observed almost roughly that Miss Lyddy hadn't better have no truck with that voodoo thing, it was soaked full o' bad luck. And to Voorhees' goodnatured surprise, Cousin Lydia had declined the gift, tactfully but very firmly: "Your friend Professor Ames will be better able to appreciate it, I think you said he was interested in anthropology," she had said. So the fetich had gone back into Voorhees' pocket. Cousin Lydia dropped the whole subject of his African experiences, they became taboo number one. The sooner the household forgot that Shad's guest had ever seen Africa, the better.

The second taboo, extraordinarily enough, was on the subject of the Morelands, Shadwell's neighbors and Voorhees' own connections. Till it came up, we had not realized how often we were in the habit of mentioning Diana Moreland.

Shadwell naturally on receiving Voorhees' wire had asked the Morelands to dinner at once, for Monday evening—his guest's first evening at Handsome Creek. They had accepted, and duly appeared: Diana a lustrous vision in filmiest black, her gaunt husband towering behind her. Dr. Richard Moreland was not considered by anyone a cheerful companion, and Voorhees, meeting this distant cousin for the first time in several years, had not been quite able to conceal the fact that the sight of him was a shock. "Why, Wing, my dear fellow," Voorhees had stammered to me in the corner into which he had fallen back, to rally his wits, "the poor chap's just a chattering skeleton! Does he never stop talking?"

Practically never, I had told him. Poor Moreland, once a world-famous bacteriologist, and now the emaciated victim of a rare intestinal disease that he had picked up during his researches in the Orient, was to all intents and purposes starving to death; he lived—if you called it living—on nothing but milk, and didn't digest that. Still, this so-called diet gave him an excuse to hold a glass of milk in his thin fingers at the table, while he nervously jingled his keys with the other hand, or played with a fork, and the rest of us took our jellied soup, and fried chicken with luscious peas, and strawberries covered with cream, and fragrant coffee. He sat there, just a bag of bones, but flippant and elegant, his glasses on his high pale nose—talking, talking, talking. He was mordant and clever, he was almost charming; you'd have liked him, perhaps, if he had been a shade less corpse-like in his pallor, a shade less feverish in his persistent flow of talk. But as it was, he made your flesh creep. As for what must be the effect of him on a lovely full-blooded creature like Diana Moreland—well, that aspect of the case you preferred not to think about.

I suspected that Voorhees, however, had given more than a little thought to the lot of his beautiful cousin-in-law, since last night. He and Diana had talked together for a large part of the evening. And this morning, while Shad and Allison and Freddy and I played a foursome over the rough local links, Voorhees had elected to make a call at Elmington. It appeared that though he had not seen Moreland, who was busy writing and excused himself, he had had an exceedingly pleasant hour with Diana under the great trees that gave the place its name. She had really had to drive him away, he said. "A very pretty common-looking child arrived, to whom she is teaching music, she told me. What a graceful charity!" And then, "I suppose she realizes the state Dick's in—that he can't possibly live very long?" After that, he had sunk into abstraction, and by lunchtime it was plain to anyone who mentioned Elmington or its tenants that Voorhees would rather talk about something else.

So, on the whole, my cousin Lydia's present choice of subject seemed an excellent one. And no one was prepared to enjoy it more than my incautious Gertrude herself. I say incautious, because she had for the time forgotten Cousin Lydia's characteristic manner of handling her tales.

Cousin Lydia began harmlessly enough. "Yes, Handsome Creek is supposed to be cursed. Or hexed. A hex is a sort of spell. What the negroes call 'cunjur.' It's from the German 'hexe,' meaning 'witch.'"

"And how does it work?" asked her friend.

If you had not known my cousin Lydia, you would have been surprised to note a trace of discomfiture in her answer. "Why, nowadays of course it doesn't work at all."

The truth is that Cousin Lydia had always had a passion for tales of disaster. Freddy vowed that her one disappointment in Shadwell, after his return to settle at home, had been his failure to supply her with the excitement of a serious accident or a deadly disease. And he further accused her of downright depression over the sad fact that the family curse was undeniably, as he put it, a flop.

Shadwell had come out of the house just in time to hear her last words. He stood by her chair, his usually grave face lighted by a twinkle of mirth. "My aunt Lydia, Voorhees, is one of those gentle souls whom our daily existence does not provide with enough material for their very active sympathies. So she hungers for recitals of suffering and blood and broken bones. If one of her fellow beings has to have a peculiarly excruciating fracture set without an anaesthetic, she can always tell you just how far his screams could be heard."

And now Isham, the immensely tall and thin old colored butler, appeared with glasses and ice and what not on a tray which he set down, saying, "I'll be right back with the soda-water, suh."

"Isham," said Cousin Lydia kindly, "how is Georgia's poor dog?"

"Bingo ain't no better, Miss Lyddy. He ain't goin' to be no better." Astonishing how, without so much as a glance at Voorhees, Isham managed to convey an impression of injured resentment. He had not forgotten the "voodoo." And he withdrew in grumpy silence.

Cousin Lydia sighed. "How they do love a 'bad sign,' poor creatures! How they love to tell me, when they drop a plate, that they never drop plates in any other house, but Handsome Creek is known to be 'onlucky.'"

"They must be having a perfect time fretting about that African image of yours, Voorhees," said Shadwell. "A regular debauch of shivers and creeps."

Ann Page gave a little gurgle. Ann Page had the most delicious young laugh that ever came from mortal throat. "You'll never guess the latest thing they are fretting about. Georgia told me, but it's not to be mentioned to Isham."

"Sit tight, then, infant," said Shad. "He's coming back in a minute with the soda!"

"I'll tell you quick before he gets here.—They're all stirred up about your terrible, terrible scar."

"My scar?" said Shadwell, looking round at her. "Oh—you mean that old place where the bull got me? What on earth do they know about it?"

"Oh, they know a lot! Isham saw you in your bath."

"The old liar," drawled Shadwell coolly, but with an angry color rising. "He never sees me in my bath."

"Oh, but one day he peeked!" Shad was facing away from us, but I thought the very back of his neck looked irritated, and so must Ann Page have thought, for she began to excuse Isham. "The other servants were deviling him all the time to do it, that's why. Georgia vows she had a vision that showed her a terribly deep scar, all red and purple, and ridged up, that was growing longer and longer endways around your ribs, like a snake.—She must have heard one of your realistic descriptions of it, Cousin Lydia! And it's well known among the colored people"—Ann Page gurgled again—"that if the two ends of a scar ever meet around you like a belt, you die. So they were crazy to know how soon it would meet!" Shad, in evident disgust, did not move or speak. She concluded, rather flatly, "But he told them the scar was no different from what it was when you were sixteen. So you're safe, after all, Shadwell."

Shad gave a short, breathless, mirthless laugh. "When was all this?"

"I forget. Not very long ago."

"And Isham thinks I'll live awhile yet, does he?"

"Don't be angry with him!" she begged. "Now that he's told them the facts, they'll forget about it." Merely the charm of Ann Page's delectable soft pleading voice would have made you understand why Freddy Gibson was out of his head about her.

Shadwell wheeled round to face the lawn, he was holding the bowl of ice, and he was as pale as he had been red. "Damn—damn—damn!" he exploded rapidly, and on each word a flashing cube of ice flew from his hand, and smashed against a tree. The bombardment kept up till he had half-emptied the bowl, and a sheet of splinters lay on the grass. "Can you beat the colored race?" he then demanded. "Talk of an elephant's never forgetting—why, there's not a negro on the place that doesn't remember and think of me as I used to be—a sniveling, contemptible, cowardly boy (oh, yes, I was, Aunt Lydia!) that used to shake all over if a cow mooed out in the field!"

Cousin Lydia said defensively: "But you were simply all nerves, you had been so terribly injured!—That child," she said impressively to Voorhees, "was a mass of blood. The bones of his left arm stuck right out through the skin, and the arm just dangled. The shock stopped his growth for a year or two. You know what he was like at school."

"Puny," said Shadwell bitterly. "Always in a funk. I tell you, my one regret about coming home to live was that people would be always looking for reminders of that boy in me! Serves me right for leaving the life I'm used to, and fit for, and settling down."

"You're an unreasonable idiot," said Voorhees lightly. "Living a perfect life here—and you want trouble."

"What he really wants," said I, "is for Handsome Creek to catch on fire, and give him a chance to go leaping up and down blazing staircases, rescuing the ladies."

"That's all right for you fellows," Shadwell said. "Nobody's peeking at *your* backs. Nobody remembers hearing your own father call you the first white-livered Dunn in history." He smashed another ice-cube, and set down the bowl.

Ann Page was annihilated by the effect of her story. Her brown eyes filled with tears. "I'm sorry, Shadwell," she said. "I'm sorry I said a word about it."

Shad looked at her, hard, for a silent moment, then, "It's all right, infant," he said.

But from that time we noticed a constraint towards Ann Page in Shadwell. Freddy's comment was: "That tale must have rubbed him raw. But he'll get over it." Freddy couldn't imagine anybody not forgiving Ann Page.

Now the screen-door creaked, the old negro was returning with a siphon. And Shad's features tightened. Nobody was saying anything, which was unfortunate, for it made it necessary for Shad to speak; he had to prove to us that he wasn't really upset. So he said, in an almost-natural voice, "You've left off the lemons again, Isham." Which only proved how badly upset he really was, for the lemons were there all the time. And his hand wasn't steady yet. The glasses clinked together.

Isham glanced at the tray, but did not presume to examine it. He said, "Yessuh. In a minute, suh," and hurried away. By the time he got back again with more lemons, protesting, "I sho'ly thought I had put them on, suh," my cousin was quite himself once more. He said, "My mistake, Isham, They're here under my nose. But leave the second lot too. Set them down." From the sudden ambiguous sparkle in his eye, I judged he was detaining Isham for a purpose. He watched him, as the old man found a place for the second dish on the tray, moving things about, clumsily, with his gnarled brown hands.

I wondered what was coming, and hoped it might not be a public rebuke to Isham for spying on his employer. Perhaps it would be only a jest. Shadwell sometimes gave preposterous orders to Isham to see if he would look surprised. "You can bring me a mug of asses' milk, Isham," I have heard him say. "Wild asses." But the old fellow was never caught. His indulgent aged smile only said, "This nonsense pleases Mr. Shadwell, and doesn't hurt me."

What Shad now asked him surprised me, it was so irrelevant. "Isham, did you bring down those old flannel trousers for Mr. Voorhees to wear fishing?"

"Yessuh."

Shad slapped a handful of loose change on the table. "Just count that over, will you, and take the coppers out. Then I'll tell you what to do with them."

The old negro stood there, tall and drooping, obediently counting the coins as he passed them from one hand to the other, and I was struck, as I so often am, with the air of patient incuriousness which his race can bring to their execution of our commands. I had no doubt then, and I have none now, that Isham's thoughts were busy with strange, befogged, and occult interpretations of Shad's order. How can any white man guess what symbolism he found in this matter of the copper coins? Into all my cousin's acts I suppose the servants read a second meaning, after Voorhees' African fetich came into the house. Whatever the old man thought or guessed about Shadwell and the copper cents, or whatever weird significance those innocent bits of metal had for him, we now know that Isham was groping his way in a tragic bewilderment, not all of it due to the fog of primitive terror around him.

"Seven coppers, suh, fo' nickels, six dimes—no, seven dimes," Isham corrected himself, running a thumb over the smooth surface of—"a coin a half-dollar an' six quarters."

"Now, Isham, try to remember. Did you ever know anybody except me that was tossed by a bull?"

"Nossuh. I don't think so, suh."

"Then I'll tell you something. Do you know what's the best lucky-piece in the world? It's a penny out of the pocket of somebody that's been tossed by a bull, like me. You can keep one of the coppers for yourself. But the other six you are to put in the hip-pocket of those trousers for Mr. Voorhees—maybe they'll help him to catch some fish. He was a pretty poor fisherman when he was at school."

Voorhees sputtered, "Of all the barefaced fictions—! I was a *good* fisherman."

Shad only grinned. "Run along, Isham," he said, "and do as I tell you." He thrust the change back into his pocket like a man relieved of care. The strained moment was over. Either his watchful scrutiny had somehow satisfied him on Isham's score; or else he had decided to reserve rebuke until a better time, and was glad to put it off. I hoped he had decided against it altogether. But I myself felt still obscurely agitated. I could not at once recover, after having heard my self-contained cousin break out with such intense feeling. How deep must those old accusations of cowardice have cut him! Much deeper than I yet knew.

We had all begun conscientiously to chatter, to show how much at ease we felt, when Voorhees lifted his voice. He was being cheated out of Miss Perryman's story, he protested. What about that curse?

CHAPTER II

As Cousin Lydia prepared to speak, "Voorhees," said Shadwell, not without a touch of affectionate irony for his aunt's benefit, "you're a lucky dog. I'd give anything to be hearing this yarn for the first time myself!" Taking up his glass of plain soda (perhaps it was because Avery Dunn had been a hard drinker that his son never touched alcohol), he walked away into the house.

"The hex was put on," said Cousin Lydia, "by a woman—a girl—who had every reason to feel herself badly treated by—well, in fact, by Shadwell's father. It's no secret, Heaven knows! My nephew, Avery Dunn, had many faults, and my niece-in-law, his poor wife—she died when Shadwell was at school—never was the woman to handle him. This other person, this girl, was a handsome, reckless creature, living down by the old quarry. The family's name was Sloap."

"Sloap," murmured Voorhees. "Sloap. Too good to be true. It doesn't sound real. I shall wake up."

"Shadwell was only three or four years old then," pursued my cousin Lydia. "The unfortunate girl died when her baby was born—a poor child who never lived to be a man, either, but was found drowned in the quarry-pool one morning. So at the time all the misfortunes really fell on that unhappy family. But though Avery always pretended to laugh at the hex, people remembered it when Shadwell ran away as he did years afterwards, and his father never saw him again. For the curse was this: Handsome Creek was never to be inherited by any descendant of Avery Dunn."

"No witchcraft about Shadwell's running away," said Voorhees stoutly. "Perhaps you don't know it, Miss Perryman, but I met Mr. Avery Dunn sometimes when he visited Shad at school, and once I saw him in a rage—

I've never forgotten it. An uglier customer I don't care to see. Why, his whole family and household ought to have run away!"

"Well, he was punished. As for the hex, he always refused to speak of it. But he brooded, and neglected the farm, and let his law-practice go to pieces. He offered rewards, he had descriptions sent broadcast. If Shadwell hadn't gone abroad, he couldn't have kept hid, such a queer-looking pale, handsome boy—there were too many things to know him by. That distinguished way his hair grows in a point on his forehead (you've noticed it, Mr. Voorhees?—just like his grandfather's portrait in the hall). And at that time, though no one would believe it now, his run-down and undersized look for a boy of seventeen. He would surely have been traced and found. So after a while everyone was sure he was dead."

"Hell for Cousin Avery," I said. "Hell being what the dying wench evidently wanted her detested lover to have."

"And did her best to arrange it for him," she agreed. "You see, Mr. Voorhees, her mother was a witch before her, and taught her—"

Here Gertrude began to look uneasily at me. We had heard the tale before, and my wife, who cannot bear any circumstantial account of physical suffering on the part of man or beast, had learned to dread the details. But Cousin Lydia had always shown a kindly willingness to omit the most trying parts of the story when Gertrude was by. So I nodded reassuringly, and murmured, "She won't forget."

But that was exactly what Cousin Lydia, intoxicated with Voorhees' rapt attention, now proceeded to do. She had called the discreditable roll of the Sloap family, including the old snuff-taking mother—herself unmarried—of the vindictive girl; also the feeble ancient uncle, a former undertaker of the village, reputed to have second-sight, and to have practiced hideous rites with corpses. These two, rejecting all assistance, had laid out the dead girl's body, and buried it—At that point, I could hear Gertrude drawing (too soon!) a deep sigh of relief; the worst of the tale had been skipped by Cousin Lydia, the danger was over.

Alas, Voorhees innocently brought it back! "Is there a ritual for putting a hex on you? Do they make a man of wax, or what? Those two old warlocks and the dying girl—what did they *do?*"

Forgotten was poor Gertrude! Cousin Lydia leaned impressively forward. "To begin with, they had a fire of coals, and they split a living rabbit open, and roasted—"

"Oo-oo-ooh!" An outraged wail from Gertrude cut her off. "Oh, Cousin *Lydia*, how *could* you, when you know it makes me crawl all over, and my stomach turn upside down?"

She was on her feet, looking greeny-white. "You ought to *tell* me when you're going to be so dreadful, and I'd gladly go away.—I'm going now, don't start again till I'm gone!" She darted into the house, leaving poor Cousin Lydia looking almost as sick herself.

"Oh, Carter, I'm so sorry! Shall I go after her?"

"She'll be all right," I said. "She'll take some spirits of ammonia, and cry a bit, and lie down. But for Pete's sake lay off of that rabbit stuff the next time she's around. It simply does her in."

Cousin Lydia finished in a brief and chastened form. "So the grandmother had the baby christened Thomas Jefferson Sloap, of all things! It was a dirty, neglected, scowling little thing, with a mop of black hair in its eyes, as rough and wild as a hawk; Avery ought to have done something for it." (Cousin Lydia invariably spoke of this temporary bearer of the Dunns' bar-sinister as "it." Sexless and ageless she made the vanished blot on the "scutcheon sound.") "And when it was killed, the old uncle came up to this house on his old trembling legs, that very afternoon. He got into my nephew's library, with his eyes rolling in his head like a medium; it was something to give you the creeps. He prophesied that Avery would get bad news of Shadwell from school. And so he did."

"I remember that time," said Voorhees. "Shad got into one of his spectacular rows with a master, and ran off. A fearful to-do it made. The headmaster, old Chalmers, had to inform Mr. Dunn. Sweet job."

"Old Sloap," said Cousin Lydia grimly, "had informed him first."

"Did Mr. Dunn believe him?"

"Of course, he swore he didn't. He kicked him out of the house, and came raging in where his mother, who kept house for him after Shadwell's mother died, was sitting with me. I was here on a visit. He said he would tell the hands to horsewhip old Sloap if he ever came back. He wouldn't say what Sloap came for, he just stamped away down the hall. But Shadwell's old colored mammy had overheard, and she came crying into my own room presently and told me."

"I should say," said Voorhees, "that the hex had worked pretty thoroughly!"

Cousin Lydia went on. "Mammy said the old man began by telling Avery he was 'marked' to hear bad news. 'I can read it there on your forehead,' he said. And Avery said, very kindly for him, 'I *have* heard bad news, Sloap. I hear that your sister's grandson got drowned in the quarry.' And started to give him some money. The old man just knocked his hand away so that the money fell on the floor, and said:

"'That isn't bad news to you, that's good news. You're glad it happened, I know you!' He was close to delirium tremens, he had been dead drunk in the village the night before. ('I guess that po' chile was drunk too,' old Mammy said. 'He was all battered up, they tell me. He had fell off the high rocks.') So old Sloap had found the drowned body in the morning, and had hauled it home, laid across the little express-wagon of a frightened child that he compelled to help him. And old Mammy said the child went home to its mother, and had a fit right there in the floor, because the body—"

"'Easy, easy, Cousin Lydia,' I said. 'Gertrude may come back.'

"So then, 'You'll let me pay for the funeral,' Avery had said. 'Pay nothing!' said the old man, and told him he had laid the boy out himself, with no help, and no thanks to anybody. All he had come for was to let Avery know that bad news was on the way to him, and that it would be about Shad. 'Your precious runt,' he called Shadwell. 'Our Jeff was worth ten of him,' he said. Imagine the insolence!" said Cousin Lydia superbly. "But—the bad news *was* about Shad!"

"Whew-w-w!" Voorhees looked at me. "What a tale! Do you really believe in second-sight?"

"Certainly I don't," I said. And added weakly: "But can you explain it? Some people said at the time that Shadwell might have written his plans to the younger boy in advance; he had sometimes played with him, though it was strictly forbidden. But as you know, he ran away just on the spur of the moment. Anyway, we know positively that he did not write to him. At least, not then."

"What do you mean by 'not then'?"

"He did write later," said Cousin Lydia. "Not knowing, of course, what had happened to the poor child. His only word home for nearly twenty years was written"—she summed it up impressively—"to a dead person!"

"Of course, that way of putting it," said Voorhees, "does give one what the Scotch so delightfully call a cauld grue! But there's no logic in it. It's just a thrill produced by Miss Perryman's technique. I am sure she could tell me the story of the three blind mice in a way that would chill my marrow."

"Well," confessed Cousin Lydia, "what he wrote was really just a card to say he was on a ship between Norfolk and New York, and was never coming back. You see, his father had thrashed him terribly the last time they complained of him at school. The postcard was brought up by old Sloap, and thrown inside the door."

"Old Sloap couldn't have forged the thing, just to be nasty? He doesn't sound a pleasant person."

"Of course we thought of that. He was capable of it. And although the postmark was quite genuine, the writing might have been anybody's. It was just a seasick scribble. But Shad really did send it himself. All that Avery could ever learn, though, was that a boy giving the name of Jones and wearing a Chalmers School cap, went north on that ship, and disappeared in New York."

"Bully for him," said Voorhees heartily. "His running away was what made him. Made him rich, made him strong, made a man of him. You wouldn't have had him stay at home, with his spirit broken? He's escaped having his father's sins visited—"

Shad's voice called to us from the hall. "Time for this fishing-party to get ready to start!"

We found my brother-in-law and Paul Allison inside in the hall as well. They were getting fishing-tackle out of cupboards. "Hi, Shad!" sang out Freddy. "Which rod for Mrs. Moreland?"

"She likes the black one," Shadwell said. "Come along, Voorhees, hurry, you can change your trousers in the library. Diana will be here any minute."

"I understand that Dick's not coming with us?" Voorhees seemed trying to keep the hopefulness out of his voice.

"Moreland? No, he's not coming. Too seedy."

"Shad," I said, "I think you might tell Voorhees about our experience with the doctor. As a connection of his, perhaps he'd better know."

"All right," said my cousin after a moment's hesitation. "Voorhees won't tell. Come along with us while he changes."

So it was in the library, with Voorhees informally and hurriedly peeling off his neat nether garments, and getting into Shad's old flannels—much too long, and needing some laughable adjustments—that the story was told. "Moreland's anxious," Shad explained, "that the matter should be kept from his wife, at least, till he's perfectly sure.—He believes he has a chance to get well."

"Get well?" Voorhees gasped. "In the state he's in?"

"He hopes so. That's what he told Carty and me."

Shad and I, driving one night, had found Moreland apparently collapsed in his car, halfway on the road to the Burnsville Hospital; and to induce Shad to drive him the rest of the way, he had revealed his errand. He was going over to get an injection of a serum which a young doctor there had worked out during a recent visit to the East; the stuff was in the experimental stage, and Moreland had desperately offered himself as a subject.

"'He does it for nothing,' Moreland told us." This was Shad speaking. "'I've no money, the crash almost wiped me out.' Your cousin the doctor was fairly babbling, Voorhees; he'd have told every secret of his soul in that moment, to get to Burnsville. 'I mean I've no money except my joint account with my wife,' he said. 'She manages our affairs—she has a head like a man, a good hard business head! But there's nothing to spare for a long treatment like this, and anyway I'd rather she didn't know. So the treatments are charity. I'm not proud.' Not proud—huh! Probably would rather die than ask his wife to make a sacrifice—especially as I'm certain there's a good deal of friction between them."

"Friction?" returned Voorhees disgustedly. "That's too mild a word. Last night I said to him how very lovely she looked in black, and I wish you could have heard the quiet, venomous precision of his answer: 'She's rather an artist in clothes. It seems that they interest her.' And then he walked away."

"As bad as that? No wonder they can't discuss money matters," I said. "Especially as no amount of money can make his recovery a sure thing. Far from it."

"I think he believes he's on the way to a cure. 'I've gained three pounds this week,' the poor devil kept saying,' said Shad. 'And haven't fainted like this for a month.' By Jove, he had been driving himself back and forth twice a week, in the condition he's in; always at night—didn't want anybody to know where he was going, till the thing was sure. Sometimes he'd stop from exhaustion two or three times on the way, but he usually got there. So, of course, we took him over, and I offered to send a car and driver for him after that, or even drive him myself, but he said he'd be all right, he was really improving. And I had to leave it at that."

"But if he goes out two nights a week, how can he hide it?"

"All that Diana knows about it," I said, "is that he has an unaccountable mania for driving around at night alone, and it keeps her perfectly mad with anxiety. She doesn't dare follow him, but sometimes, when she can't stand it, she goes out to look for him, in an old station wagon they keep for errands. She told Gertrude she found him once, doubled over his wheel in a dead faint; he had just been able to pull over to the side of the road before he passed out. Of course, that night he had to go back home with her, he didn't get his injection."

"And naturally," said Shad, "one has fits of thinking she ought to be told, promise or no promise. But since it's impossible to guess from her manner with him whether she would be glad or sorry if he died, and yet equally impossible not to suspect that she might be glad—for God knows his manner with her is worse than glacial—well, on the whole, Carty and I decided to tell nobody. Not even Gertrude."

Voorhees stood there in the hitched-up trousers, a grotesque and pensive figure, sunk in thought. "And she knows nothing of the chance that he may yet recover," he said in a queer brooding voice. It didn't take much penetration to see that the unuttered thought behind the words was: "And how will she feel when she knows?"

CHAPTER III

When we came out into the hall again, the young people were ready. Allison was going along with us, for half an hour or so; he would then leave us, and take the five-fifty train to see his guardian. Voorhees had advised against his accepting Freddy's offer to drive him the fifty miles he had to go. "We both think the train is best," Voorhees had said. "Anyway, he'll be back before half-past nine."

Presently, an immensely long and impressive olive-green roadster, shabby, but clearly once of notable price, spun up to the door. Diana Moreland, dark-eyed and lovely in a pale-yellow knitted frock, sat at the wheel with her husband by her. As she descended, he slid over into her place without stopping the engine. "He never cuts it off," said Shad in Voorhees' ear. "Diana's here a lot, she's mighty sweet to Aunt Lydia, and he brings her up to the door and drops her; then he always talks for a bit, nineteen to the dozen—as you see—to my aunt." Moreland was in fact the one person whom my cousin Lydia would descend the front steps to talk to. She would sigh, "Poor fellow!" and trip down to the bottom step, and they would both talk at once, above the low humming of the engine, for neither of them had any idea of listening. Then Moreland would make his cadaverous bow, and there would be a rising purr from the car, and he would glide away. As he did now.

Our own cars were now being brought round by my cousin's chauffeurs. Freddy sang out, "Hey, everybody! Get a move on." And "Gertruu-ude!" caroled Ann Page to the figure of my wife at the window upstairs.

Gertrude came running down. She and Cousin Lydia exchanged a silent kiss of peace that buried the rabbit episode, and gave each other those little feminine pats that mean, "If you won't bring the subject up again, I won't either." Very sweet I thought they looked together.

We were taking the two roadsters, Shadwell's and mine, plus Freddy's car. Voorhees and Diana had been enjoying a turn in the rose-garden, but now they were back, and Gertrude, who was to be their driver, gravely explained to Voorhees that he had to take his raincoat because Cousin Lydia had descried a small cloud in the west. "You'll find," she said with twinkling eyes, "that she has put a pair of smoked glasses, your trusty knife (in case you want to whittle), and two boxes of matches (in case you lose one) in the pocket! Don't you feel like a Sultan, or something?"

They drove off first, the young people followed, and Shadwell and I, in his dark blue Daimler, brought up the rear.

My cousin had thrown all irritation off, he was in high spirits—why should he not have been? The day was fine though hot; we were on our way to an hour of peaceful sport, or at least the pretense of it, in pleasant company. Every prospect pleased. Diana Moreland, the handsomest woman in Frisbie County, was going with him and Voorhees in the steadiest boat, as per specifications in advance by Cousin Lydia. And that same Voorhees, his school-friend and old companion, was hour by hour warming his heart with a most gratifying admiration and envy of his personal qualities and his lot. The man who says he doesn't enjoy being admired in his own house simply lies.

Shadwell never talked much, but that afternoon, I remember, he whistled softly as he drove. Only the weather troubled him a little, it threatened the crops. No real sign yet of the drought's breaking, just a dry blistering heat that even as we drove made us glad to have our shirt-collars open at the throat. "I've got on just two garments, above my socks, and it's two garments too many," he grumbled genially.

Then we rounded a curve in the road, and there was the little river. Ordinarily it was but a muddy stream, but the long drought had made it clear as glass. Low in its bed, it slipped drowsily along. Freddy and Allison were waiting for us with the boats; Ann Page was in the canoe that they had chosen, and Gertrude and I took another. Voorhees, having helped Diana into Shadwell's boat, stopped, and thrust a hand into his pocket. "What was it you said to me about money, Paul?" He brought out a roll of bills.

"That I'd be obliged if you'd lend me some, sir. I'm short.—That dingy outside one is quite all right. I shall be changing it." But the aged bill that Voorhees stripped off—dog-eared, creased, and lacking a corner—proved to be a hundred, and Allison waved it away. "Oh, sorry! Couldn't use it!

Haven't you a twenty?" Among the ones and fives and tens a lone twenty was found, and Allison pocketed it. "Glad I'm not trimming you too close."

"Lord, no!" said Voorhees. "What do I want of money?" He grinned at Shad. "I'm a blissful parasite!"

Gertrude and I made for the farther side of the river, where there was shade under the big sycamores. Shad's boat and the young people's canoe turned downstream. "Don't let Mr. Allison forget the time," Gertrude called after Freddy. "He has to take his train."

By five-thirty the heat was less stifling. Gertrude and I had long since decided not to fish; we had tied up to a drooping branch, and let the boat swing gently in the shade. I dozed a little, and Gertrude, peerless wife that she is, let me alone. Not until she perceived that a sound of distant voices coming up the stream had partly roused me, did she begin to talk.

"I firmly believe," she said, "that Diana Moreland is the unhappiest woman I know."

"Why, I was just thinking"—I said—"that is, I remember thinking—say, what time is it?"

"You've been asleep," said my wife, "just twenty-five minutes. And enjoying it!" She gave me that indulgent and maternal, and yet not-too-maternal smile, which always means that I have been snoring, and that the snores have not annoyed her, because they were mine. It isn't every woman who can in the same breath inform you that your sleep has not been silent, and also bring about a three-inch expansion in your chest. She went on, "What was it you said you were thinking?"

"Why, that Diana was such ripping good company! She gets even Shadwell talking, she was doing it just now. As for Voorhees, since dinnertime last night, he's hypnotized. He told me he had forgotten what a charmer she was. She's the last woman I'd call a flirt, but she certainly makes 'em sit up and notice."

"She's a grand sport," said Gertrude. "She does her best. She keeps it up wonderfully. But she's getting less and less able to keep it up for long. More and more given to dropping silent, with eyes that don't see anything. Of course, she wakes up when you speak to her; in a minute she's her old flashing marvelous self again, she's all there. But never for long! Where is it she goes away to, when she gets that look in her eyes?"

"Maybe she goes away to the place where we try to look over the edge, and see the future," I said. "The question is: Is she afraid that Moreland won't get well, or is she afraid that he *will?* The latter, I should say. But anyway, thank Heaven, the look isn't there this afternoon."

"That's where you're wrong, my lad. This afternoon Diana has given out—given up—as I never knew her to do before. She's gone home."

"But she and Voorhees and Shadwell," I protested, "went *that* way." "That way" was downstream, away from the automobiles, and also away from Elmington.

"Darling, much water has flowed downstream since you dozed off! Ten minutes ago, Diana passed us, walking on the side of the river away from the road. Going upstream, towards home. She didn't see our boat, down here, under the trees; she felt unobserved and alone. And she had that look in her eyes."

"That doesn't sound," I said, "as if Shadwell and Voorhees had exactly behaved like knights of the Round Table. Letting her walk, in this heat!"

Gertrude laughed. "Dear innocent, do you still believe that any two men, or any two hundred men, however chivalrous, can escort a woman who doesn't want to be escorted? Diana Moreland wished to be alone. And that, you may be sure, settled it."

"Then why did she come fishing at all?" I demanded.

"Ah, I can't tell you that," sighed Gertrude. "How do I know?" She looked at me uncertainly, she had the air of preparing herself for a plunge. "Carty, darling, there's something I made up my mind an hour ago that I wouldn't tell to a soul on earth—but you know how it is! I've simply got to talk. And I'll ask you a question first: of all the possible sorts of things that give you a feeling of strangeness and creepiness when they happen, what is the creepiest?"

"Well," I said, "wouldn't it have to be something bizarre and unprece- dented—monstrous—"

"No, Carty! The thing that chills a person's blood is exactly the opposite of what you are trying to say. It's the shock, when you are quietly expecting something quite familiar, of suddenly finding that it isn't there at all! Like going up a staircase that has always had eleven steps, and walking into empty space after the tenth one.—That's the best comparison I can find for something that happened this afternoon."

"There was something you expected to see this afternoon, and didn't?" I said. "Whatever was it?"

"Not expected to *see* this time, Carty. Expected to *hear*. You know how you always, always, always hear Dr. Moreland's engine going? Well—it had stopped."

"You're nuts. Moreland's engine never stops," I said. "It positively didn't this afternoon. I'd have noticed."

"Yes, it did stop, my dear. Not the first time he came. The second time." I simply stared at her. She said, "He came back."

"But he didn't come back! And couldn't have come if he'd wanted to, for just as soon as he pulled out, all three of our cars were moved into the circle and filled it up. After Moreland was gone, he stayed gone."

My wife asked, "Do you remember the position of our bedroom?"

Our delightful corner room, allotted to us by Cousin Lydia, who is quite laudably soft about Gertrude, was much the best bedroom at Handsome Creek. Its front windows faced towards the oak grove, across the entrance-drive; the side windows overlooked, beyond the garden, the sweeping curve of the drive's disappearance round the end of the house, towards the distant gate to which Handsome Creek presents—not exactly its back, but the less important of its two fronts. In that room of ours, a lady adjusting her hat at the dressing-table, in its well-lighted angle, had a west window on one hand and a south window on the other. Her vision swept an arc of some two hundred degrees. So when Gertrude now went on, "He didn't come back by the drive," I had to realize that she was in a position to know.

She told me that as she sat putting on her hat, she heard the light humming of a car coming up on the right, outside the hedge, where there wasn't any driveway at all—nothing but the slope of the lawn. And glancing out, she saw what had happened, and why. Moreland had returned, and looking down from above she recognized in his hand the yellow silk jacket of Diana's frock. This he must have discovered in the car before reaching the gate, and instead of coming back the way he had gone, he had elected to turn off on the grass, and make a complete circuit of the house, driving on the sun-baked turf that was so dry and hard after the long drought that the tires of even a heavy car could do it no harm. Almost soundlessly he had come up to the outer curve of the hedge, meaning perhaps to call out to us, and toss the jacket over. His hand had half-lifted the soft mass of silk. Then Gertrude suddenly missed the purr of the engine. He had stopped it.

"There he sat in that silent car, Carty, which was hidden by the hedge from everybody but me. You and the others could just have seen his head over the top of it, I suppose, if you had been looking, but of course you weren't. And he wasn't looking at you, either. He was looking across the hedge and across you, looking past you, and past the corner of the house. And naturally I turned away from the front window, and towards the window that was on the garden side, to see what was interesting him so."

I remembered now. Diana had been showing Voorhees the roses; they had been out in the garden while the rest of us were fussing with our preparations.

My wife saw the recollection in my face, and nodded. "They were there. In sight of him and me, but out of sight from the portico. She had her hand on Mr. Voorhees' arm, and his hand was over it, and I'm sure she was crying."

I gave a long, thoughtful whistle.

"And then," said Gertrude, "the yellow jacket dropped over the hedge, without a sound, on the grass border inside, and that emaciated head began to slide quietly backward and disappear. He just loosened his brake, you see, and let the car coast backward out of sight down the slope, away from the house, till even from upstairs I couldn't see it any more. Then I heard him softly start the engine; and he drove away with hardly a sound over the grass just as he came. It was simply uncanny, darling!—As if Diana hadn't troubles enough!"

"Well, if you come to that, Moreland also has troubles enough," I began, feeling disposed to stand up for my sex, "without seeing his wife holding hands—"

Gertrude raised a warning finger. "Sh-h-h! The others are coming!"

The sound of voices and of oars that had wakened me was by this time indeed very near, almost upon us. Teetering around the bend below us appeared another craft, not Shadwell's boat, but the three-seated canoe, in which Freddy, Paul Allison, and Ann Page, doubled up and almost unbalanced with mirth, seemed to be courting a bath. The small craft swayed violently as they approached, they were laughing and chattering as Allison and Ann Page unsteadily wielded the paddles, and shrieked their glee in response to some recital by Freddy. He sat looking backwards over the way that they had come, and his illustrative gestures played no small part in their very evident danger of upsetting. Still convulsed, they came alongside.

"Oh, dear! Oh, dear!" panted Ann Page, wiping the tears from her eyes, "why do you have to take that wretched train, Paul Allison?—Gertrude, we had to walk out on the best show of the year, just round that bend, because a train leaves at five-fifty! Can you bear it? We had to row on—"

"And on—and on—" chanted Allison. "And leave all the fun behind!"

"Why, you thankless woman!" cried Freddy much outraged, "you carried with you the best part of the fun, which was *me!* Me, telling you every darn thing that was happening behind your ungrateful backs! Me, doing a Graham MacNamee—"

"He did, Gertrude, he did!" almost sobbed Ann Page, hysterical with glee. "He'd say, 'Now, folks, it's an even chance that Shadwell will tip out of the boat— No, he's caught himself! He's swatting at the hornets, and I think he's swearing and laughing at the same time, and Voorhees is so weak with giggling that he can't do a thing.'"

"Those two solid citizens," said Allison, "were acting like a couple of boarding-school kids. We had just come abreast of them. Mr. Voorhees had cut open Mr. Dunn's shirt-collar, behind—"

"With his little hatchet—I mean his whittling-knife that Cousin Lydia made him bring along to catch fish with—can you *bear* it?"

"Yes, he cut it because he insisted a hornet had gone down, inside—"

"And Shadwell," gurgled Ann Page, "said— Oh, Freddy, you tell them!"

"Shadwell said, 'Damn your eyes, Voorhees, you're just letting 'em in!' They were both swatting, and waving their arms, and rocking the boat. It was a scream."

"Especially,' Allison said, "as I don't believe the things were hornets at all." He pulled out his watch. "Gosh, Freddy, I must get along."

The canoe slid away. Ann Page called back to us over her shoulder. "Of course they weren't hornets, folks, they were man-eating tigers, and they had eaten Diana! At least she was nowhere to be seen. And when we asked politely what they had done with her, Shadwell began to scowl at us—and of course he had hiccups too, by that time—" She began laughing again, "Oh, Freddy—"

Freddy made a horn of his hands. "He was still trying to keep Voorhees away from his shirt-collar, too—and he said, 'She had a headache, and, besides that, she positively had to see the raspberry woman.' Now, folks, I'm sure you'll agree with me that that's an intriguing alibi. Diana Moreland, the mystery woman, leads two gentlemen into an ambuscade of hornets or man-eating tigers as the case may be, and escapes on the pretext of seeing a raspberry woman! Well, all I can say is that I'm sure you'll agree with me this is going to be one of the most wonderful mysteries of all time—" They were turning the next bend, and Freddy's voice trailed off.

At the same moment the third boat of our expedition rounded the lower curve, coming on slowly. A single figure was pulling the oars. My cousin Shadwell, alone.

CHAPTER IV

"Hello," he hailed. "I hope those young lunatics get that train! Voorhees is quite sufficiently upset already; if Allison misses it, he'll have a brainstorm."

"Why, they said that you and Voorhees were having a perfectly riotous good time with a hornet's nest or something," I told him. "Where on earth is he?"

Shadwell sniffed. "The time stopped being so good when he got stung on the hand! He wrapped it up, and made me put him ashore. Said he'd take my car, and find a doctor. Sounds sort of childish, but he's still a bundle of nerves, and a sick man. Did you see him go by?"

I had indeed seen through the trees the figure of a man going along the road, from which at this point the river curved away. It might have been Voorhees, or it might not. My cousin's tone was matter-of-fact, and defied you to look upon his deserted state as a joke, but his controlled handsome face had a look as near to sheepishness as I had ever seen it wear. Shad wasn't a person to get "rattled," but he was plainly in the position of not knowing what it was all about. And I did think it a bit hard on an exemplary host to find himself so conspicuously left in the lurch. To be sure, his companions had left him singly, and not in concert, they had even made their separate departures on opposite sides of the stream, but I wasn't sure that this made matters any better.

Shad rowed on ahead of us to the landing-place, and we paddled after. My roadster stood there alone, the dark-blue car had disappeared. So I climbed into the rumble with the baskets, and Gertrude drove us home.

"I don't think the afternoon was a wild success, if you want my opinion," murmured Gertrude to me, as we preceded my cousin into the house.

Shadwell doesn't seem to care, probably he just thought it was funnier than ever when poor Mr. Voorhees got stung. And it really is a bit silly for a grown man to dash off for first aid in that excited fashion! Shad's right, of course. One person in a party throwing fits is enough. But what with this and that—the heat, and the hornets, and the look on poor Diana's face—I wish we had stayed at home!—Shad, I love you with those ravelings sticking up at the back of your neck."

Shad, grinning ruefully, said, "It was a perfectly good silk shirt, doggone it!"

"But why so modest, even if it's torn?" Gertrude asked. "Aren't you roasting in that coat? I don't believe you'll ever be really *Southern* again, and—oh, sort of flexible and who-cares—you know what I mean. You've lived with those British colonials too long."

Suddenly Cousin Lydia pounced upon us in the hall. "What's the matter with Mr. Voorhees?" she demanded.

"Hornet-sting," said Shad laconically. "Doctor."

Cousin Lydia bridled. "It couldn't have been very painful, for Isham tells me Mr. Voorhees came back to the house, and went out again, before you got here. He must have come straight from the river, and let the hornet-sting take care of itself."

Shad said, with a puzzled look to Isham, "How long was Mr. Voorhees in the house?"

"Jes' long enough to change his clo'es in a hurry, suh."

Shad looked thunderstruck. "On his way to see a doctor? Of all the idiotic performances—! Which way was he driving when he left?"

"He warnt drivin', suh. He left the car."

"Left it? You mean he walked?"

"Yessuh."

"Then he hasn't gone far," I said. "Do you suppose he had the bright idea of consulting his cousin Dr. Moreland? Moreland would love to be asked to tie up a hornet-sting!"

Shad said, "We'll telephone and find out."

The Morelands' maid said that Mr. Voorhees had called at the house some time ago and had seen no one except herself. "He was driving, too," said Shad, putting the receiver up, "so he must have stopped there on his way from the river. The question is: Where has he gone now?"

"One more mystery," I said idly. I left Shadwell looking in the evening paper for the weather forecast.

"Hey, Carty!" he called after me. "Good news! It says rain."

When we assembled for dinner, an hour later, and learned that Voorhees would not even be back to dine, Cousin Lydia looked stricken. "I was sure Mr. Voorhees was back already. I heard the radio."

"I'm not surprised that you thought it was Voorhees," said Shad. "Isn't he the world's worst radio-hound? Absolutely dependent on it when he wants to cerebrate. Can hardly write a letter unless the thing's going.—I'm sorry I raised your hopes, my dear Miss Perryman. For about five minutes I myself was prosaically listening to—what was it?—oh, yes, to the Assistant Secretary of Agriculture. On hogs." She began to lament her friend's defection, but Shad said: "Now, Aunt Lydia, let the man live his own life! Just because I don't dare draw a breath without your consent, you mustn't expect the same of everybody. Voorhees said over the telephone that he'd be back in time for Allison's train. In other words, before a quarter past nine."

"But it doesn't take a whole evening to tie up a hornet-sting, my dear Shadwell! And I thought perhaps when he telephoned—" Cousin Lydia was gentle and deprecating, she didn't want Shad to be annoyed, but she meant to know just as much as he did. "Isham mentioned that he had called up from somewhere, just after six. Didn't you think to ask him—?"

Shadwell said, with exemplary patience: "I didn't ask him anything whatsoever. He's my guest, but he has not signed a contract to eat every meal at Handsome Creek, or to leave his address when he does otherwise." He slipped his hand under Cousin Lydia's elbow. "Dinner's ready. Come along."

"Forget the wretch, Cousin Lydia," said Ann Page, descending the stairs in a cascade of white chiffon in which she looked so lovely that poor Freddy was positively pale. "You're learning one of the saddest lessons of life: that we just have to let them love and ride away!"

In spite of everything, however, dinner that evening was a very pleasant meal. Both at table and later, over our coffee, Shadwell seemed determined that Cousin Lydia's pleasure should not be spoiled by Voorhees' defection. For once, my silent cousin actually talked. And so amusingly did he mingle teasing and deference in his manner toward his successfully beguiled great-aunt, that those hours still constitute in my mind, as I look back upon them, what might be called an occasion.

The first stage of what Freddy called Shad's treatment for a broken heart was genealogical. My cousin astutely began to talk "family," and in two minutes Cousin Lydia was busy correcting his mistakes. This had been in fact his method, since his return home, of getting quite a local reputation for knowing state history and genealogy. Gertrude had said: "I've watched you, Shadwell, and you certainly have one characteristic of a great man: you can put things over on the world. I hear people say you know every branch of every family tree in the southern Atlantic seaboard states. How do they get that way? What really happens is that somebody consults you on a knotty point, and you look wise, and get as far as, 'Let me see—' when Cousin Lydia takes the word out of your mouth, and finishes the subject. Sometimes not until midnight, but she finishes it!" And Shad had retorted: "But you'll concede, my dear, that even a complete ignoramus, who for three or four instructive years had had the words taken out of his mouth in that manner by my aunt Lydia, would end by being a darn sight better authority than most of the people in this room. And since my aunt won't let me talk, some day I shall write a book!"

So Cousin Lydia was now in her element. And before the end of the meal, Shadwell had maneuvered her even farther; we had reached her dearest subject of all: physical disaster and disease. He was encouraging her in quite a comfortable state of worry about Diana and the headache that had been her excuse for leaving the river.

"We'll telephone her," said Shad, as we rose from the table, "and ask how she is.—You do it, infant," he said to Ann Page. "Tell her some of us will come over and play bridge with her. Do her good to be amused."

I remembered that this was Tuesday, one of the evenings when Moreland made a trip to Burnsville, without the knowledge of his wife.

In a tone that was partly jesting and partly serious, Shad went on, "I wonder if you can remember her telephone number?" Ann Page's adoration of her lovely new friend was already a family joke.

"*Diana's* number? As if anybody could forget!" she returned.

"I'll believe you if you can call her in the dark."

"All right. Listen!"

She darted across the corridor, into the deep dusk of the library; we heard her call the number. "You win!" Shadwell shouted to her.

"A lot of good it does! Number's busy."

"Too bad. But—stop a minute. Hold everything. Will you call the veterinary for me, like a good child, while you're waiting? He has a party-line, 97-W. Ask him to come up again."

"He has already said the dog is dying, Shadwell," said Cousin Lydia.

"A few more words from an authority," said my cousin, "may yet convince our Senegambians that Bingo is dying of plain poisoned meat, and not because the powers of darkness have crooked their finger. Georgia has got them worked up to the point of believing that all the plagues of Egypt are setting in at Handsome Creek."

That was at half-past eight, dinner being later than usual. At half-past eleven that same night, when the sheriff had gone home, and we were talking rather shiveringly of the ease with which any intruder could enter the library by one of the long windows, and hide himself, and bide his time, all at once Shadwell exclaimed, "And only three hours ago I sent Ann Page into that room in the dark, alone!"

But at the time no one thought anything of that. We were not jumpy about little things. We hadn't begun to start at small noises, and look backward over our shoulders. That came later. At the moment we were as placid a group as you could ask to see, moving out of the dining-room, just as Ann Page was calling Elmington again. We heard her say, "Is that you, Diana, darling?"

At Handsome Creek, on summer evenings, we do not leave the lights burning in any rooms that are not occupied. There are too many moths and gnats. So it was in a pleasant semi-darkness, between high windows still palely bright with twilight, that we left the lighted hall, and passed on towards the billiard-room, pronounced by Shad the coolest place to have our coffee. The night was inordinately still and dry and breathless; the great storm that was to break on us at midnight, and end the drought and heat, was not yet stirring beyond the Blue Ridge. The air felt exhausted and dead.

We turned the billiard-room lamps on, but left the drawing-room still unilluminated, a broad strip of soft gloom between us and the rest of the house. I remember how fresh and cool Ann Page looked from a distance, when she came out of the library after using the telephone, and I watched her coming towards us down the corridor, crossing the wide bright hall and the dim drawing-room, with the vaporous white folds of her frock moving softly in and out around her feet as she came; and yet when she reached us I saw that around her face the soft rings of hair were wet and sticking damply to her forehead, like a child's. "My word, it's hot!" she said.— "Diana's feeling better. She says to come along. She's alone."

At the word "alone" Shadwell and I had exchanged glances. Moreland would be far on the Burnsville road by now; he would be driving fast and exultantly, filled with that hope of getting well, of starting life over again, about which he had told her nothing. Humming along in the moonlight—a swift car with a smiling death's-head at the wheel— My slight *frisson* was all for the wife to whom in her ignorance, he would come home, bringing his hate or his love. Which would be worse?

The coffee went round. Old Isham wore a downcast and martyrized air; he had incurred Cousin Lydia's rebuke for using the vacuum cleaner in the forbidden afternoon hours, when all proper cleaning should be over. ("I was so glad to find something to scold him for," she said. "He needs to have his mind taken off of Georgia's tantrums.") He served us with a certain meek glumness, and the dull abstracted gaze of one whose mind is elsewhere.

My cousin said, "Isham, I want the evening paper. Not the morning one. From the library."

"Yessuh." But the old fellow still stood without moving. Shad repeated, with the look of questioning scrutiny that I had noticed once before, "The evening paper, Isham. It's on my desk, right under the lamp. I want both sections."

"Both sections. Yessuh." Fully roused, Isham moved off briskly. The errand successfully done, he said in a low voice, "Bingo—he's dead, suh. Kin I go now?"

"I've just sent for the veterinary for him again. I'm sorry it's too late," said Shad. Followed by our compunctious murmurs, the old negro hurried away.

It may seem strange that we should have been affected by nothing more important than the death of a dog. But old Isham's gaunt retreating back looked somehow very pitiful! Even lighthearted Freddy sounded subdued, as he asked, "Who's making up this card-party?"

Gertrude, Ann Page, and Freddy himself were the only possible three. Cousin Lydia did not play, and Shadwell wanted to be at home when Voorhees came. As for me, I duck bridge whenever I can, and Gertrude is a merciful wife. So, the card-players having left us, I took up a novel, and

Shadwell, tossing away the evening paper, challenged Cousin Lydia to her favorite game of backgammon. By this time it was a quarter to nine.

The heat hung heavier and closer. Cousin Lydia said, "Rain before to-morrow! Do you notice how clearly we hear the train?"

This particular phenomenon served us instead of a weather-glass; when sounds from the railroad to the east were distinct and plain, always a storm was brewing. And tonight a distant puff-puff was audible from very far away.

"Allison's train," said Shad. "Yes, we're going to have a storm all right."

Cousin Lydia was for sending a car to the station. It was too hot a night for Allison to be allowed to walk up, as he had planned, she insisted. But Shadwell said, "Let the chap alone, Aunt Lydia. He knows what he wants to do. If you ask me, he wants to come in quietly and see Voorhees before he sees anybody else." The train whistled nearer. "He'll be here in a few minutes now— And there, by George, comes Voorhees himself! Sharp on time."

The sound of a screen-door at the far end of the west corridor opening and closing, and the appearance of a figure that seemed to pause and blink at the light, impressed me vaguely—very much as the talk of my companions had done—through the sulphurous haze of the crime-story I was reading.

Shad called out, "Is that you, you old pirate!" and went hospitably towards him.

Voorhees stood motionless, at the far end of that same long vista down which Ann Page had come towards us with her white draperies fluttering round her feet. And though at the time I did not define it to myself, there was something unsociable and unnatural and slightly disconcerting in the way he kept his distance from us. He made no friendly gesture of greeting, even to Cousin Lydia. Shadwell had to go all the way; Voorhees did not speak till Shad was beside him, close to the library door. Then I heard his voice, fatigued and low, saying something indistinguishable to me (my attention was enthralled by Edgar Wallace's villain with the chloroform cone as he bent over the girl), but sounding unmistakably glum and depressed. He said only a few words.

"In the library?" said Shad, sounding surprised. "Why, of course. There's paper and ink and everything. Come in, come in."

Their two voices diminished, and I ceased to be distracted from the doings of my villain (who was bending lower still) until I became aware of

Shadwell again, saying over his shoulder, politely but not warmly, as he came out, "Well, I hope you've got everything you need."

Some hours later, when we were trying to get to sleep, and couldn't, I asked Gertrude, "Do you think it would have made any difference if Shad hadn't closed the door?"

At first he had left it open, he had actually started down the corridor. But he stopped and went back, and with some half-laughing remark to Voorhees about the radio, pulled the big double leaves together. "Now you can go to it!" he called as they closed.

Gertrude thought that the shutting of the door had made no difference—and anyway I mustn't suggest the idea to Shad! "Besides, how do you know that Mr. Voorhees wouldn't have shut it the very next minute himself, if he had a secret appointment?" she asked. And the question was reasonable. Everything about Voorhees' actions that evening had been secretive and mysterious. Nothing seemed more likely than that he would have closed the door.

When Shad rejoined us, I thought he looked quite as baffled as the rest of us looked eager and curious. "He's writing a letter, he'll come in presently," he said, in a dissatisfied and apologetic tone.

Then began the drag of waiting till Voorhees should deign to emerge and explain the unceremoniousness, the almost rudeness, of his behavior—including this latest vagary of shutting himself up to write letters, the minute he entered the house. Cousin Lydia showed the effect of the suspense; she grew more and more fidgety. And thoroughly disliking any conduct that made that dear little lady fidget, I grew cross. As for Shadwell, any feeling that he may have had showed itself only in an uncharacteristic restlessness. He couldn't settle down to backgammon again.

"We've got some other games," he said. "Where are they?" Cousin Lydia didn't know. They ought to be somewhere around. "Haven't I seen them in the hall cupboard?" he asked. That wasn't where they belonged, she said, but lately you never knew what Isham would do next.

Shadwell strode off to see, it was plain to me that any excuse for activity was welcome. I watched him open the cupboard door. Half-inside, he called back to me, "What did I tell you, Carty? Listen to that!"

"That" was the distant radio bursting into song.

Shadwell returned with several games. "I don't care for that radio singer," said Cousin Lydia.

"That's where you show your uncultivated taste, ma'am," said Shad. "That is Columelli, the new tenor who's coming to the Metropolitan in the fall."

"She shows pretty darn good taste," I said. "He's rotten."

"All right, run along and throw a dead cat at Voorhees for turning him on. I'm willing."

This excursion into musical criticism lasted just long enough to fix in our minds the fact that Columelli was singing at nine-five.

Shad stood turning the varicolored cardboard boxes over, half-heartedly, still with the slightly restless air of a man who feels he has an explanation coming to him, and can't settle down till he gets it. "Jigsaws—anagrams—parcheesi— They don't look so good to me." He made several trips to the cupboard for others, but the result was the same. He didn't care for them. The end was that everything went back.

While he was making up his mind, Cousin Lydia admired the moon from a window, and wondered why the veterinary was so slow about going home. "He's just starting. I suppose it must be the veterinary," she said. "No, he has turned his lights off again, he isn't going. Those headlights look very feeble to me; that's dangerous. There was such a nice young druggist in town who lost both legs and a piece of his jawbone—"

Once or twice while Shad's process of elimination was going on, we heard the radio stop, and Cousin Lydia would turn round and prick up her ears, and look hopefully down the corridor. But each time the music started again.

"What's the man doing in there?" my cousin grumbled. "Why can't he settle down, and get through?"

Suddenly I heard Cousin Lydia say, quite sharply for her, "What is it, Georgia?"

Dimly visible through the long window-screen were Georgia's white cap and apron. The rest of her melted into the night. The girl was pantry-maid nowadays instead of chambermaid, because her father had asked that she be placed under his eye; but he did not seem to be looking after her this evening. "Miss Lyddy, I'm skeered."

"Go and find your father." Cousin Lydia was kind but firm. Georgia, well known to be an hysteric, had no business anyway at this end of the house when her work was done. She should have been over at the servants' cottage. But Isham slept in the house, downstairs beyond the kitchen, and usually he could calm her down. "Go find him."

"Miss Lyddy, listen. I saw a ball o' fire come down fum heaven and burst under them trees by the gate."

"You saw the veterinary's car. He turned the headlights on, and then off again."

"Naw'm. De vetternary didn't have no car. His car's broke. He come up with his brother-in-law, an' walked back."

"Well, it was somebody's car."

"Naw'm. I'd 'a' seen two lights."

My sofa was near enough for me to enter the conversation without moving. "Did you see two lights, Cousin Lydia?"

"It might have been two lights, or one. The car was sideways to me. I saw a long bright flaring streak—" With her hands she outlined a funnel-shape.

"And from the servants' cottage they saw it head-on. A 'one-eyed cat,' of course," I said. "One bulb burnt out."

"There, Georgia," said Cousin Lydia. "Mr. Carter has explained it. I suppose the brother-in-law came back, that's quite simple. Now you go to bed."

"I'm skeered, Miss Lyddy. Mr. Vo'hees he's shet up in the liberty prayin' to that ole Affercan god."

"Oh, by Jove!" I said to Cousin Lydia. "He left it on the desk in there when he changed his trousers, and that's started 'em! I'm like Shad: what won't they think up next?"

Shad himself had come nearer, he was irritably playing with the ornaments of the mantelpiece. Now he came to the window. "Go to bed, Georgia, didn't you hear Miss Lydia?"

"Yessuh. I'm goin'." The two white blurs that were cap and apron retreated. "But Pharaoh los' his firs' born when de Lord's angel struck by night! De angel an' de sword—de angel an' de sword— De Lord tole me to walk all de way roun' dis house, an' I'm a-walkin' roun'—walkin' roun'—" We heard her pass through the rose-garden and go by the portico; after that her voice was inaudible.

Shad had put the boxes back. "Looks as if Voorhees was good for all night in yonder," he said. "Well, my dear Miss Perryman, backgammon it is!"

And the distant music went on and on, as if it would never stop again. I was just slipping into a gentle doze on my sofa, when Shad exclaimed, "Let's have a change what do you say, Aunt Lydia? How about Russian Bank?"

Cousin Lydia agreed, but there were no cards out on the card-table where there should have been the usual two packs. She began looking about. My cousin said, "Carty, will you look in the library? There are some in a box there."

But he reckoned without Cousin Lydia's love of indulging us all. "Poor Carter! He's tired. Let him alone, Shadwell. I'll get them."

She was fairly out of the room before she stopped speaking, and Shadwell and I were left looking at each other—I with the sheepish, startled look of the half-awake, and he with a glance of strongly adverse criticism, as he said, "Confound you, Carter, I'd have done it myself if I'd thought you'd let Aunt Lydia get ahead of you."

"Oh, she likes to wait on people," I said flippantly—Heaven forgive me! "She waits on you all day long. Why shouldn't I get spoiled a little? Why should you be the only—"

I never finished. Cousin Lydia stood swaying in the doorway, her little trembling hands clutching the curtains at one side. Her mouth opened and shut, but she did not make a sound.

CHAPTER V

The card-table was overset with a crash, Shadwell sprang forward with outstretched arms that just succeeded in catching Cousin Lydia as she fell. "See what's wrong, Carty! Something has scared Aunt Lydia almost to death."

I dashed into the hall just as the front door burst open, admitting our three card-players, who had returned surprisingly soon. They entered gaily, but the sight of me wiped all the mirth from their faces. "Lord, what ails Carter?" I heard Freddy exclaim. I had the sense to wave the girls back. Freddy came pounding after me down the corridor as I ran.

The library door stood half-open, jazz-music was pouring out of it now. And over Shad's desk, still adorned with the African fetich, a strangely humped and muffled shape drooped forward from its seat. The formless outline of a head, darkly draped, was bowed upon the blotter; it had about it a dreadful suggestion of the attitude of prayer. Next moment I made out the lower portion of Voorhees' figure. The upper half was swathed in his own raincoat. And under the spot, where his left shoulder-blade would be, stood out the wicked bloody haft of a knife. "Good God!" said Freddy in my ear.

The one thing I could think of to do was to stop the radio. In the sudden stillness I heard Ann Page calling Cousin Lydia's maid downstairs, and the confusion of voices on the stair-landing as the woman met Shadwell coming up with Cousin Lydia in his arms. Freddy and I had no more than verified our certainty that Voorhees was dead—stabbed to death behind closed doors and in front of an open French window—when Shadwell was with us, the two girls trembling behind him.

It was characteristic of Shadwell that he did not say a word. When Freddy said, "We mustn't touch anything," he just nodded. He stood darting piercing glances about the room—at the window, the desk, the still form. I said, "I'll call the sheriff," and he nodded again. But Voorhees was fallen all across the wire of the desk telephone. "I'll have to call from the pantry telephone," I muttered.

As we all moved out into the corridor, Shad exclaimed, in a startled voice, "Where's Allison?" We all looked at one another. Where *was* Allison? The train had whistled half an hour ago. Allison should have reached the house in ten minutes. Could he have come in, and gone straight up-stairs? No, the person Allison would have wanted to see at once would have been Voorhees, of course. My eyes followed Shad's eyes to the long open windows. A walker coming up by the quarry path would have approached Handsome Creek from that side—

All at once, Allison was there among us, as we stood huddled together in the corridor. He appeared from no one knew where, but certainly not from out-of-doors. He said, "What's the trouble?"

Shadwell in the same breath asked sharply, "Where have you been since you came home?"

Allison flushed. "I've been in the p-p-pantry," he said.

An extraordinary expression came over my cousin's face. His dis-pleased reaction to Allison's unaccountable words—unaccountable in a young man just back from having dinner—was written on his brows, for-biddingly ridged. It emphasized the unpleasant queerness of this sneaking entrance by a young man under a cloud. A very small and minor sort of cloud, of course, but a cloud just the same. A young man too who knew there was a certified check upstairs, but did not know that the rest of us knew it also. Shad repeated, slowly, "In the pantry, you say?"

An ominous quality in Shad's voice made Allison take a step backward; he fairly trod upon Isham just emerging from the pantry door with some-thing in his hand. There was a crash and a warm smell of coffee.

"There goes yo' cup and yo' las' sandwich, Mr. Allison!" Then the look of our strange and petrified assemblage struck the negro, as it had already struck Allison. "Ain' nothin' wrong, is there, Mr. Shad?"

Shad eyed the scattered bread and meat, the smashed china. He re-peated automatically, "His last—?"

"Mr. Allison was pretty near through, when he heard y'all out here in the hall, suh!"

It was now Shad who looked white. He passed a hand over his forehead. "Allison," he said, "you'll make allowance for my tone to you. If you had gone straight to Voorhees when you came from the train—"

"But I wasn't on the train! I got a lift home. I have been home half an hour, in there with Isham. I wanted to get something to eat quietly, and not disturb anybody.—My God, Mr. Dunn, what *is* wrong?"

In Shad's face an expression of helpless rage was struggling with something like humiliation. I said to myself that Shad would have liked to kill somebody, here and now, about this outrage that had happened in his house, and there was nobody to kill. It was plain to me that his first angry impulse had been to see guilt in Allison's ambiguous entrance on the scene, and I thanked Heaven for him that in his excitement he hadn't said so. He passed his hand over his forehead again, and said heavily, "You might have been in time to save him."

"To save whom?" Allison looked about him, he was at the library door in two strides, and his croak of horror made Shadwell catch him by the arm, and call, "Here, Isham—brandy!"

Ten minutes later, we all found ourselves collapsed into chairs round the table in the dining-room. Shad had wired to Washington for a detective. Allison had telegraphed his guardian, and the sheriff was on the way. Freddy and Isham reported no footprints discernible on the terrace and the hard ground outside the library windows; and no finger-prints on the knife, which had been grasped in a fold of the raincoat. "So there was no spatter at all on the murderer's clothes, either," said Freddy. "What's more, it was Voorhees' own knife."

Now it was Allison, revived by the brandy, who was feverishly asking questions. When he heard that Voorhees had dined away from Handsome Creek, he started. "I wonder—" he was beginning eagerly, when he was interrupted. The sheriff, with the coroner's physician and a couple of deputies, was shown into the room by Isham, and took charge.

He spoke with respectful sympathy to Shad. "This is a terrible business, Mr. Dunn. We'll have your account first, of course." But Allison had sprung to his feet, and stood biting his lips, eager to speak. "Just a minute!" the sheriff said, civilly enough. "It's a matter of form, of course, but I have to ask that no one leave the house. Good idea if for the present nobody leaves this room."

The answer was the violent scrape of a chair on the other side of the table, and a figure sprang toward the door, hurling aside the deputy who stood in the way. The screen-door to the west porch slammed, almost before the empty chair toppled over on its back. Allison had disappeared.

CHAPTER VI

Twenty minutes later, all the facts that the household could muster seemed to be in. Every one present had been examined, including Isham, the only servant on duty downstairs since Voorhees' return. So far, the sheriff had not summoned Georgia. Her impression that Voorhees had been praying was only too easy to explain. An alarm had been sent out for Allison.

"It's clear that Mr. Voorhees' murderer, whoever he was," said the sheriff, dispiritedly, "had a perfect chance. The door was shut, the windows were wide open, the radio was on. The unfortunate gentleman had his rain-coat with him, it seems (of course there's a big storm working up), and on his return had dropped it by him on a chair; perhaps the knife stuck out of the pocket, handy. He hasn't been robbed, it wasn't a murder for robbery. So it must have been a murder for ill-will. We've got to find his enemies."

Shadwell said, "I could have sworn he didn't have any."

"Not even that young man who ran away?"

"Allison's behavior hasn't been that of a guilty man," said my cousin positively. "I believe he'll come back, and I'm sure he'll be able to explain— In the meantime, we'll scour the neighborhood for marauders."

"I wish," said the sheriff, "that we knew why Mr. Voorhees stopped the radio twice. Could he have been listening for somebody from outside—expecting him? And was it a friend—someone that he took to be a friend, I mean—or an enemy?"

Shad said: "Mr. Sheriff, suppose you let me speak to the other servants. The cook and the maids sleep in a separate cottage which has a distant view of the north side of the house. I'd like to find out whether any of them saw a visitor approach the library windows."

The sheriff approved. While Shadwell was gone, we moved poor Voorhees' body into the sun-room; we covered it and locked the doors. Except for this removal, the library remained as we had found it.

By this time my cousin was back again. "The servants who were over there say they saw no one go in the library window, which possibly means only that they didn't look at the right moment. And they didn't hear the house radio stop—or hear it start either, for that matter. They have a radio of their own, which goes all evening, of course, and they are instructed to keep their windows down on this side when it is turned on. But they astonished me by saying—" He paused. "See if this strikes you as it struck me! You realize that, though the storm is piling up, this is still a moonlight night? So bright that anything moving on the lawn could not have failed to be visible to a person looking out from inside the library, supposing (this is the point) that the library itself was dark! Well, the significant thing is that Voorhees apparently not only stopped the radio several times in order to listen—we ourselves know that, we heard it stop—but also, just for a minute or two, according to the servants, put out the light! He did that, they say, at least twice. It may have been a signal. Something prearranged. Or he may have done it in order to keep watch for somebody on the outside."

"Or keep watch *against* them," the sheriff said. "Maybe it comes to the same thing."

Some formless guess at the feeling of a hunted man at bay, alone, and waiting, consciously perhaps, for his doom—waiting within reach of the help he dared not call for, or so it seemed—gave me the "cauld grue" down my spine that poor Voorhees himself had so merrily spoken of, only that afternoon. All of us drew a little closer together. And all of us started violently when the deputy in the doorway gave a surprised exclamation, and Allison staggered past him, dripping with sweat, and dropped into a chair.

"I thought," he panted, "that I could run down something, but I haven't got anywhere. I've only thrown a girl into hysterics. And yet she ought to know. She *ought to know!*" He pounded the table with his fist, and glared round at us. "Oh, this is simply hell!" His head dropped on the table, and he broke into heavy sobs.

When he got quiet, he asked meekly for some more coffee. ("Never mind if it's cold, Isham.") Those sandwiches had been all his dinner he said. He looked utterly done. Oh, yes, he had seen his guardian this evening, though too late and too hurriedly to dine with him. That part was all right. He had settled his own business. It was something else he had to tell us about.

The beginning was that he had missed the five-fifty train. Ann Page and Freddy had dropped him at the station, and driven away, not knowing that the train had already gone. He had waited some minutes before making inquiries. He had then walked over to the bus-stop, and found that a bus would pass in three-quarters of an hour, After a while it occurred to him to telephone Professor Ames of his change of schedule. "So I walked round to the drug-store, where the booths were, and went into one. There was somebody talking in the next booth, a man with his back towards me. And in a minute I recognized his voice. It was Mr. Voorhees."

Allison had sat as still as a mouse, he told us. He hadn't even tried to get his connection. He didn't want Voorhees to know that he was there, that he had been careless enough to miss the train; it made him feel such a fool. And so, quite innocently, he had become an eavesdropper.

"I heard him finish his talk with somebody—they were having quite a row—and hang up. And I heard him take the receiver off again, and that time he called Handsome Creek and had his little talk with you, Mr. Dunn. Just saying he hadn't let you know he'd be out for dinner. And then he hung up and walked out of the store. And I let him go." He gulped and went on. "You see, the first telephone talk, the one that was going on when I came in, hadn't seemed to me any more important than the second one. He was giving somebody a calling down, all right, but it appeared to be a business matter, and he hardly sounded angry, only contemptuous, as if he despised the person he was talking to. But now, I'm wondering whether the man at the other end of that wire mayn't have been the person who killed him!"

"What were they talking about?" the sheriff asked.

"I wasn't really listening. In fact, I was trying not to listen. But Mr. Voorhees was accusing the other fellow of some pretty flagrant sort of fraud. I heard him say it was 'perfectly transparent,' as if he were talking to a yellow dog. Apparently he had been awfully loyal to the other fellow, too. Talked about 'sticking to you.' The chap had been taking an unfair advantage, though, somehow, and Mr. Voorhees had found him out."

"Unfair advantage of Mr. Voorhees?"

"I don't know. But he was pretty sour about the situation, whatever it was; he called it 'all wet.' And the worst of it was, I think he made some sort of appointment to meet the scoundrel."

"Here?" demanded Freddy. "Tonight?"

"I haven't an idea," said Allison unhappily. "The other man said something, and must have been naming a time and place, for Mr. Voorhees just said in a haughty way, 'That will do perfectly,' and hung up the receiver Wait a minute, though! Before that, he had said, 'Of course, I'm leaving at once.' So if they made an appointment, it must have been for tonight."

"Unless they were meeting at whatever place Mr. Voorhees was leaving for. But anyway, it's a cinch," said the sheriff complacently. "We'll just trace that call."

"That's the worst of it—you can't," said Allison.

The immediate tracing of that call had been Allison's own object, he told us, when he had bolted out, half an hour before. He had easily found the telephone girl who had been on duty at six-twenty; he had trailed her to her home, and then to a movie, and had dragged her out. But she could not remember the number of the first call. She simply couldn't. Of course no record was kept of local calls. "We stood there in the street, she and I and her date, and wrangled, and all at once she began to cry, and then her date wanted to fight me. The end of it was she was so upset that I suppose now she can't remember her own name."

The situation was considerably complicated by the fact that at six-twenty the operator had been impatiently waiting to change places with her successor, who should have come on at six, but arrived late. There had been high words between them. Girl number one had her date, and wanted to get home to dress. And in the general acrimony and confusion and back-talk, several switchboard connections had been made, which had wholly failed to register in her memory. She did remember calling Handsome Creek. "But the other number could have been anything," Allison groaned. "A private house, a garage, another pay-station—she simply does not know."

For Allison's benefit we now repeated such information as had come out. He was struck when I told him about Georgia. "Probably she saw Voorhees through the window," I said. "She told us he was praying, and we paid no attention to it thought it was just her religious obsession. But he must already have been dead."

"You don't suppose—" Allison began.

But we had been over all that. "Georgia is left-handed, and not at all strong," said Shadwell. "And it was a vigorous right-hand blow."

That ended the evening's session. The sheriff prepared to lock up the library till morning and leave a deputy on guard in the west corridor. Shad sent the girls upstairs, and the rest of us helped in the locking up. Allison and I were closing one of the long windows and drawing the curtains, when I noticed that the hem of the curtain, sweeping along the floor, was carrying something with it. I picked up the little crushed greenish wad of paper, and smoothed it out. I gave an exclamation of surprise. It was a crumpled hundred-dollar bill.

CHAPTER VII

Allison pounced on it. "See!" he cried to us all excitedly. "This came out of Mr. Voorhees' pocket!"

"But he wasn't robbed," Freddy said. "His roll is in his pocket now, this minute. He has his watch and everything."

"This identical hundred was in that roll this afternoon," said Allison positively. He held up the dingy bill, all of us could see that it lacked one corner. "It's the one he offered to lend me, down by the river. *You* saw it, Wing."

"Then we've got something to go on!" Shad said.

"I'd like to know what you think we've got," said Freddy. "Looking for finger-prints on that rag would be a joke."

And the sheriff agreed with Freddy. "This is no ordinary robbery, Mr. Dunn," he said. "That bill just makes things more mysterious, it seems to me."

Gloomily he locked the library door, and the dining-room and pantry doors opening into the corridor; and having seen a cot placed for the deputy behind a wide screen set up to shut off the corridor from the hall, he gloomily went home.

I found it hard to get to sleep that night and it seemed to me that I had no more than closed my eyes when I was awakened by a long peal of thunder. The threatened storm had burst over us, and for three-quarters of an hour it murdered sleep. The rain lashed and poured, the thunder and lightning were continuous, and long before the storm had rained itself out, the air was cooler by twenty degrees. Actually, one needed a blanket.

Gertrude was up and rummaging for extra covers, by the faint diffused twilight that was going to be bright moonlight if the clouds broke, when I heard her give a startled exclamation. She was staring at a moving light

63

on the wall, that was certainly neither moonlight nor lightning, and in another moment we were aware of sounds outside that were not part of the diminishing storm. "Why—that's from a headlight at this hour! There's a car coming up," she said.

I got up, we looked out of our window. A small car was swinging round in front of the portico. It stopped, a man got out, cap in hand, and lifted a black face; he was a negro. "Thisher Mr. Dunn's house?" he asked softly. When I said yes, he turned towards the car, and helped a small frail muffled figure to alight, which promptly doffed its hat; we saw a rumpled mop of white hair.

"I hope you'll excuse my arriving at this hour—that is, if it's as late as I think it is," the figure said, with an indescribable mixture of punctiliousness and vagueness. "I was considerably delayed in a number of ways. Professor Ames."

Gertrude exclaimed to me: "Oh, poor thing, it's Paul Allison's guardian, and he's something like eighty years old. He must be simply dead!—Go let him in. I'll be down."

Five minutes later, in the billiard-room, after Gertrude had apologized in despair, "The pantry's locked, I can't even get you a glass of milk!" we found ourselves being surprisingly fed by Professor Ames on sweet chocolate and biscuits, produced by his servant Robinson from his luggage; and we were being put through a courteous and deprecating but very searching interrogation.

We must have looked a quaint trio: Ames, five feet two in his boots, and perhaps one hundred and fifteen pounds all dressed, with the white crest that made him resemble a damp but undaunted cockatoo; Gertrude, rather like a sleepy little boy, with her curly red hair and her neat jade-colored bathrobe; and my tousled self in pajamas. And all of us munching chocolate bars.

The professor had no idea of wasting time. He waved Robinson off to get some sleep in the car. ("He's used to it, my dear madam!") As for himself, he felt no need of sleep. His ward's friend and kind advisor was lying murdered in this house, and Professor Ames was here—very vague, very affable, but somehow seeming even more determined than if he had been disagreeable and brisk—to know the reason why.

He was disappointed to learn that the library was locked. But he wasted no time in regrets; he settled down to extracting from Gertrude and me an account of everything that happened before the murder was discovered. "I am a scientific man, Mr. Wing," he said. "The methods of the laboratory are tedious, but they are the only methods I know."

And so that interrogation began, of which I have already told.

The time of the murder naturally was fixed, by its nearness to train-time; also of course, by the radio programme. Ames said, "I take it that this household is not fond of the radio, since it is banished to the library."

"Cousin Lydia dislikes it intensely," I said. "Listening isn't her strong point. And Shad doesn't care for music. Sometimes the young people use the radio to dance to. But today, except when Voorhees had it going, the only time it was turned on was when Shad was listening in the gloaming to a discourse on hogs."

The professor wanted the whole history of the evening. He wanted to know who had been of the party, and just how they were occupied. Nobody occupied at all, was that it?—except Miss Avery in the library telephoning for a few minutes, and Mr. Dunn reading the paper.—Then after having coffee, Mrs. Wing and the young people had gone out to play cards, and Mr. Wing had read a novel? But apparently someone had been playing cards here also, at this table. Oh not playing cards, just waiting for some cards to play with? He got the story of Cousin Lydia's horrifying visit to the library.

And before that?—He heard about the backgammon game and all the other games, and the train-whistle, and Voorhees' return, and the appearance and conversation of Georgia (whom we explained to be left-handed), and the radio. And before that?—We worked backwards, always backwards, to Voorhees' absence from dinner, to Allison's account of the telephone talk, to Voorhees' call at Elmington, to the fishing party, He congratulated us on our remarkable memories. Now might we return to the radio programme, please?

We were pleased to show off our good memories again. Columelli had been singing when it started, Shad had told us so at the time. "The new tenor that's coming to the Metropolitan," I said. "And if you ask me, the Metropolitan's stung."

Ames looked about. "There would be an evening paper somewhere, with the programme?" We unearthed it at last, badly crushed, from my pet corner of the sofa, and smoothed it out. "Sorry!" I said. "When I settle for an evening with Edgar Wallace, I'd sit on my grandmother's hat, and not notice!—There's the column you want, sir." But he was staring into space, looking so abstracted that I thought he was going to sleep on our hands. "Perhaps you'd like to go to bed, Professor Ames."

"No, no, I was only thinking, Mr. Wing. I happen to know that Mr. Voorhees was intensely musical, and now you have told me that his first selection turned out to be of a disappointing nature. Wouldn't he have changed to another, then, unless—"

"I get you! Unless he was deep in a most important conversation."

"Or else was so interested in looking and listening for someone—" He put the newspaper into his pocket. "Another thing: Mr. Wing, I note that, from your excellent post of observation on the sofa, you had a view of the entire length of the house. Did you change your position? Did you move from that sofa corner, after you began to read?"

"You don't know my husband, professor," said Gertrude. "Give him a detective story, and he's riveted to his seat. I think he waved a hand to poor Mr. Voorhees when he came in, but I'm not even sure of that."

("And to think," was Gertrude's comment, seven days later, "that he was up to his tricks with us already that very first night! Pretending to be interested in one thing, and pumping us about something altogether different, all the time!")

It was after that that Ames had started talking about the analysis of phenomena. But by this time I was atrociously sleepy, and the professor himself was beginning to blink. The clock had struck three. My wife, already half in love with the little man's quaint ways and old-fashioned politeness, exclaimed that he wasn't to sit up a minute longer. She offered him the spare bed in Freddy's room, so that poor exhausted Allison need not be disturbed.

Amenable to this suggestion, he rose stiffly. "If you really think, my dear Mrs. Wing, that your brother will not object to sharing his room with me—"

But before she started to lead the way upstairs, she had one more thing to say. "There's a question you haven't asked, Professor Ames. The sheriff didn't ask it either till he was reminded—but I'm surprised at *you*."

He gave her an appreciative glance. It was plain that my wife and the little professor were going to get on. "I didn't need to ask, I had guessed the answer, my dear lady.—There wasn't any hornet-sting."

That completed Gertrude's subjugation. "I might have known!" She shepherded him towards the stairs, with many apologies because no separate bedroom was available. Naturally one couldn't offer him Voorhees' room. She twittered over him all the way upstairs.

CHAPTER VIII

Next morning while I was shaving, Freddy entered in the wake of Gertrude's breakfast-tray. "Well, sister dear," he told her with a broad smile, "you parked a two-ring circus in my room last night!" He settled himself on the foot of her bed. "Your boy-friend began the day by asking if I minded his sending for his Man Friday, a mahogany-colored person named Robinson. So Robinson appeared, looking like a well-disposed gorilla—I swear his arms are five feet long. And darned if those two don't spend all their time throwing things at each other! No hard feeling about it, you understand! Little Ames solemnly explained that Robinson is catcher for the colored ball-team at home, and that when he has to be absent from ball-practice, on duty with his employer, he likes to keep his eye and hand in by catching small articles that are thrown his way from time to time. So Amesey indulges him—the old boy almost puts a curve on the military brushes, you'd be surprised, he quite kept me dodging—but slippers aren't so good. My child, that pair are worth buying a ticket to watch! It's a game, and they play it by the rules. But the professor says he also makes a point of surprise-throws from time to time throughout the day, to keep Robinson on his toes. I tell you, I hope he stays a week! A person like me, sojourning in what the newspapers will undoubtedly call a house of death, needs a ray of sunshine. And I want to see Shad's face when he starts throwing the ash-trays."

"Quit the kidding," I said. "You're making it up. That old boy's a distinguished ornithologist or something, and he's eighty years old."

"Not a day over seventy-five!" said Gertrude, with spirit.

"Well, he may be a hundred and seventy-five, but he's as bright as a button, behind those wistful helpless looks of his," declared my brother-in-law. "And I'm not making up a thing. Ask Allison if you don't believe me. He said to me last night, 'I'll be glad when that old guardian of mine gets here. You look out for him—he'll surprise you. As long as he's just kind of moderately wool-gathering and wandery-eyed, he's normal. Normal for *him*, that is. Meaning that his mind isn't working more than a hundred per cent faster than most people's. But if he ever begins to look like an absolutely total loss—just a shade more vacant than a vacuum—as if he had been born sub-normal, and then dropped on his head, if you get what I mean—then that old boy has stepped on the gas and really started *thinking!*'"

"Ass!" I said. "Cut the nonsense, and come to breakfast.—Better hurry down, Gertrude. Shad's detective arrives at nine-fifteen."

We found Professor Ames down before us, looking neither very bright nor very dull, but quite like any other old gentleman of seventy-five who has been up three-quarters of the night. He was getting on beautifully with Shadwell; they were discussing the habits of South American birds. Just as we came in, Robinson, who seemed already to have established himself as assistant in the dining-room, appeared with the announcement, "Mr. Hoopes."

"Show your stuff now, professor," said my irreverent brother-in-law. "—Ready, Robinson?—Put a curve on a biscuit, Dr. Ames."

Shad's eyes opened, and the professor, in some confusion, explained his little eccentricity, which, however, he had no intention of publicly indulging, he said, when on a visit. But to Robinson's relief, Shad declared that the household would find nothing unbecoming in a moderate amount of ball-practice from time to time. Nor would Freddy be appeased, even on this grim morning, till a biscuit had shot across the room to be engulfed in Robinson's brown paw. My cousin then went out to meet Mr. Hoopes, who was no other than the detective from the Washington agency,

Hoopes was a ruddy, non-humorous, literal-minded person, energetic and bustling. (Gertrude pursed her lips the first minute she set eyes on him.) He took down Shadwell's statement, he cursorily viewed the library; he then expressed a wish to go through Voorhees' personal effects. On this errand Shadwell and Allison accompanied him. After a short time, they came down together again to the dining-room. Hoopes had something in his closed hand.

"I have here an article," he said, "that was in a small box apparently thrust hastily into a bureau drawer in Mr. Voorhees' room. It might be his, it might belong to some careless member of this household. It's not the sort of thing most men travel around with." He held up a small gold frame, the size for a miniature, set with several magnificent diamonds. There was a glass in it, but no picture. "This is a very valuable article," he said. "Does anybody recognize it?" Evidently neither Allison nor Shad had done so.

Every face in the room but one was blank. It was Ann Page who gave a little gasp of recognition, and then clapped her hand over her mouth.

The detective said, "It's yours, Miss Avery?"

Ann Page said, "Yes," in a suffocated voice, and came forward to receive it, with a deeply scarlet face. She looked so odd that there was a surprised little silence in the room; then a vague and puzzled old voice quavered, "I wonder why you are taking the trouble to lie about it, Miss Avery."

Allison jerked round incredulously towards his guardian, who had a faraway look that startled me it brought back so vividly the descriptive words of Freddy, sitting this morning on the foot of Gertrude's bed: "More vacant than a vacuum." And Allison had now a swift change of expression, as if he recognized it too. But Shadwell had also turned; he began with ominous calmness, "Just what do you mean, Dr. Ames, by—"

He got no farther. The plaintive yet somehow commanding old voice said: "Don't waste time looking at me, Mr. Dunn. Look at Miss Avery. She is not accustomed to lying, she cannot do it without turning crimson.— Why don't you tell us the truth, my dear?"

Ann Page, now crimson indeed, with brimming eyes, covered her face with her hands; the tears ran through her fingers.

The professor said, "The truth never hurt anybody, Miss Ann Page."

She sobbed, "It's Diana's. I suppose you'll find out, anyway."

"Diana's?" Hoopes inquired, with interest.

"A neighbor of ours. A Mrs. Moreland," Shad said in a level voice. "There is no doubt some perfectly simple reason for its being where it was."

"Mrs. Moreland," repeated Hoopes portentously. "An old friend of Miss Avery's?"

"I've known her just three weeks," said Ann Page defiantly. But I know her well enough to be sure she's the splendidest person, the finest—" She choked. She insisted that she had had no reason for lying. "It was just an impulse," she said. Then, more firmly: "I think she has troubles enough without this! I don't know how the frame came to be in this house, and that's all I have to say."

Hoopes dropped the subject, he turned to other matters, he seemed to forget her existence. But he saw her presently slip out of the door, though I thought I was the only one that noticed it. He gave her just time to get her connection on the pantry telephone, then he was after her. As he swung the pantry door open, Ann Page was saying in what any fool could tell was a brightly artificial voice, for the benefit of possible listeners, "I knew you'd be glad to know what had become of it."

Hoopes said sharply, "Just a minute there, Miss Avery!" She answered sweetly and distinctly straight into the mouthpiece, "Certainly, Mr. Detective! I'm just about to hang up." Then to the murmur audible over the wire, she responded, "What's that, darling?" Hoopes took an exasperated step forward as if he felt strongly tempted to snatch the receiver out of her hand. But she said quickly into the telephone, "No, it isn't, dear. It's gone!" And hung the receiver up.

Hoopes held the door open for her to pass him, and said grimly: "You think fast, don't you, Miss Avery? But maybe you've done us more good than harm—that is, if your friend Mrs. Moreland asked you what I think she did: whether or not the miniature was in the frame."

Ann Page gave an astonished nod before she could stop herself, and Hoopes emitted a grunt of satisfaction. After that full-bodied hearty sound, the deprecating voice of Professor Ames sounded thin and flutelike, as he asked, "And did you notice, Mr. Hoopes, that Mrs. Moreland thinks even faster?"

"—And what do you suppose he meant by that?" I demanded of Gertrude, when I went upstairs to tell her about the excitement she had missed. She was just powdering her nose.

"Why, he meant that Diana was warned by Ann Page's saying 'Mr. Detective,' and had cleverly asked that question because she thought it sounded innocent, of course. The real problem is: innocent of *what?*—I'm ready, darling. For Heaven's sake, let's get downstairs. If I miss any more I shall die!"

Hoopes went briskly to work. Soon all of our household and staff at Handsome Creek had been examined. Voorhees' strange retirement into seclusion immediately on his return had been described; also the behavior of the radio. "Did the stops come when a number or a station was signing off?" he asked us. We told him no. The music quit in the middle of a selection, and then picked up the same thing again, farther along.

Allison in his turn testified as before concerning the substance and the approximate time of the mysterious telephone call. Nothing came out that differed from the testimony obtained by the sheriff, except an intimation

from some of the negroes that the Morelands' servant "knew something."
"Grapevine telegraph!" whispered Freddy. "Not one of them has been allowed to leave the place, and yet I bet they know ten times what we do."

The only humor of the hearing was supplied by Isham, when he was
asked to verify the time of Voorhees' telephone call for Shad.

The old man gave his testimony with an air of pretended embarrassment, because it involved the confession that he had been disobedient to
my cousin Lydia's orders. But anyone could see that he was pluming himself no little on the fact that it was precisely this disobedience that enabled
him to answer so positively for the time, and gave him his value as a witness. He had noticed the hour, while Shadwell had not.

The telephone rang, he testified, just as he was at his broom-cupboard
door in the pantry. "Gettin' out the vacuum cleaner," he murmured with
an apologetic roll of eyeballs towards Cousin Lydia. A voice that he recognized as that of Mr. Voorhees had asked for Mr. Shad, who was then
in the library. Isham had duly announced the call and had seen Mr. Shad
take down the receiver. "I heered him say, 'What-all become o' you, you ole
heathen?' Mr. Shad says, jus' lak that, talkin' into the telephone. So I knew
I was right about its bein' Mr. Vo'hees. That was near 'bout twenty pas' six."

"How did you happen to notice the time?"

Another deprecating roll of eyeballs in Cousin Lydia's direction. "Because I run right back to the pantry to git the vacuum cleaner, befo' Miss
Lydia would come downstairs fum her nap that she takes befo' dinnah, an'
ketch me at it." Seeing Hoopes look puzzled, Isham went on in a tone of
some condescension, as of one explaining the ways of persons of position
to an outsider: "At Handsome Creek, they ain't no noisy cleanin' supposed
to be allowed after lunch-time. Jus' real quiet cleanin', like with brush-an'-
pan. But when Mr. Shad's been fishin' he cert'n'y do track dirt on the hall
carpet—I know him! An' of co'se I shut the do' so's not to bother Mr. Shad
with the noise. But Miss Lydia hadn't gone up to lay down yet, she was out
in the garden. So she ketched me all right."

Even Hoopes had to smile. "And what clock did you look at, for the
time?"

"It was jes' right after Miss Lydia come in that the hall-clock said half-
pas' six."

At this point Shad called attention to the fact that this was a grandfather's clock with chimes. There was no chance of mistake.

Georgia's account of the ball of fire interested Hoopes much more than it had anyone else, so far. Of course it was a car with one headlight. He walked out and examined the ground, and found no more indications than the rest of us had done. "The weather last night was just made for trespassers," he said resentfully. "The soil was baked so hard that you could drive a car anywhere—a car did I say? You could drive a ten-ton truck!—and it wouldn't leave a sign. And there was the moonlight on top of everything else. No headlight needed." But he was inclined to agree with the sheriff that no visitor bent on murder would have driven his car on such a bright night into his victim's very grounds. "Too risky.—Still, maybe he killed him on the spur of the moment. Just got mad, and struck."

He next went into the very early return of the card-players from Elmington. "Why was that?"

"Mrs. Moreland's headache got worse again," said Freddy. "She called the game off, and asked us to get her some medicine from the drug-store in the village, and leave it on the hall-table. She was going to bed."

"Get her some *medicine?* And this a doctor's house?"

"Come, Mr. Hoopes," retorted Freddy the irrepressible, "don't you know a preacher's children never have any morals, a candy-maker's children never have any candy, a dog-catcher's children never have any—"

"Oh, do be sensible, Freddy!" begged Gertrude.

"All right, all right, Light-of-my-Tents!—so we got the medicine, Mr. Hoopes, and left it."

"Did you see Mrs. Moreland again?"

"Mrs. Moreland," said Freddy with dignity, "had gone up to bed."

"Was the house dark?"

Freddy paused, apparently weighing the advisability of telling Hoopes that he was fed up. So it was Ann Page who answered, "Downstairs it was all dark, except the hall."

"That arrangement presumably meaning that the doctor hadn't come home yet?"

"I—I suppose so. It was only a few minutes past nine."

Freddy took up the word again. "Upstairs Mrs. Moreland's room was lighted dimly, and her bathroom brightly. We inferred a bath, and came discreetly home."

His first investigations ended, Hoopes became thoughtful. He sat balancing the diamond frame in his hand. "If you'll go over with me, Mr.

Dunn, after lunch, I'd like to give this back to the lady. And ask some questions there."

Ames mildly said that, as an observer vitally interested in every aspect of Mr. Voorhees' last day on earth, he would like to go along. I could not help remembering that Gertrude last night had told Ames something that was known to no one else except me: how Moreland had seen his wife standing in tears in the rose-garden with her hand on Voorhees' arm. "And perhaps my presence would attract less remark," said the professor, "if Mr. Wing accompanied us also."

So the four of us drove over together to Elmington. Hoopes asked if we minded making a quick start. "I want to catch them still at the table," he said.

What Hoopes really wanted was a chance to examine Diana's mulatto servant in the presence of her employers. His tactics worked. Moreland and Diana had not left the dining-room. Diana spoke a word of encouragement to the flustered maid when Hoopes explained he wished to question her. She herself showed no uneasiness, As for Moreland, he sat with his lean knees crossed, jingling his keys, dry and expressionless as a mummy, and not much healthier-looking. His usual inhuman vivacity had given place to an equally inhuman reserve.

The maid said that about a quarter to six, the afternoon before, Mr. Voorhees had called at Elmington, apparently in haste, and asked for her mistress. Being told that Mrs. Moreland had not yet come home, and that Dr. Moreland was busy in the laboratory, he had left something for Mrs. Moreland, with the message that he would see her later in the evening. He had, of course, never returned.

"Did Mr. Voorhees ask for Dr. Moreland, when he heard that the doctor was at home?"

"No, suh. He said he wouldn't interrupt him."

"What was the article he left for Mrs. Moreland?"

"One of these-here automobile maps, suh."

A queer offering to a lovely lady, I thought.

"Had anything come up later about the call or the map?"

As a matter of fact, the maid said, Dr. Moreland had come into the living-room later, sometime after the caller had gone, and had rung for a glass of milk. Seeing the map lying on the table, he had received an account of the call. She had left Dr. Moreland in his big chair, looking at the automobile map, and sipping his milk.

"Did Dr. Moreland look disturbed by having missed Mr. Voorhees?" Hoopes seemed to think he was being vastly subtle.

"Dr. Mo'land don't never look disturbed." The answer drew a wintry smile from Diana, but not a change of expression from Moreland.

Hoopes having finished with the maid, we passed into the living-room.

Then Diana, being asked, said that she had not spoken with or seen Mr. Voorhees since she left the fishing-party at the river.

"Have you any idea why Mr. Voorhees called to see you, Mrs. Moreland?"

"Apparently to lend me a road-map of New England."

"Why should he have done that?"

"I suppose as an allusion to something we must have talked about, though I can't think what it could have been. But everybody discusses motor-trips more or less. And not always with strict attention to what the other person is saying.—The map is here." She took it from a table, and held it out.

Hoopes satisfied himself that nothing was written on it. "Then Mr. Voorhees had not suggested taking a trip anywhere with you?" he said.— "And with Dr. Moreland also, of course!"

Shad looked ready to punch the fellow's head, and might even (I believe) have done it, if there hadn't been something ludicrous in such an action by an outsider, while Moreland continued to sit silent, folded up like an emaciated jointed doll into one of the deepest chairs I ever saw, and with his mind apparently anywhere except upon the conversation— twisting the cord of the telephone beside him, drumming with his fingers, playing with his cigarette. But Diana only said with tranquil aloofness, "Dr. Moreland and I have not for a long time made any plans of that kind."

I heard Ames mutter something that sounded like "Brava!" But Hoopes wasn't sensitive. He shifted to another line. "Last evening at nine o'clock, I understand, Mrs. Moreland, you broke up the bridge-game, pleading a return of headache. Then, when your friends had left, you went out for a drive in your small car." So that was what the "grapevine" had meant!

For the first time, Diana hesitated. Moreland, not looking at her, said, "Carry on, by all means. Why not?" She was very pale. She said: "I was uneasy about my husband. He has a habit of night-driving which he sometimes indulges beyond his strength. Once—" She looked apprehensively at Moreland.

"It's quite all right," he said, with his eyes on his cigarette-smoke.

"Once I found him insensible, beside the road in his car, which fortunately he had been able to stop. Since then—occasionally—I go to look for him."

"Did you find him last night?"

She said, in a trembling voice, "The time I have spoken of was the only time I ever found him."

I had to drop my eyes from her pale face. My glance fell on Professor Ames' hands, they were knotted tightly together. Ames did not believe Diana. Not any more than I believed her myself.

Suddenly Hoopes said, "Do you recognize this article, Mrs. Moreland?"

It was the diamond frame. Moreland's spasmodic motions ceased. He continued to look at nothing, apparently, but he sat quite still. Diana replied, "That is something that used to be my grandmother's."

"Whose picture was in it?"

"My own. A miniature that was painted soon after my marriage. For my husband."

"And Dr. Moreland lost it?"

If it is possible for a perfectly motionless person to become more motionless still, that is what happened to Moreland. Diana said, "Probably it was stolen."

"You did not, by chance, give your miniature to anybody?"

"I did not."

This time I said to myself, "She's telling the truth now, no matter what the professor thinks."

"You have no idea how it came to be in that drawer in Mr. Dunn's house?"

"I have no idea."

And for some reason I couldn't explain, I was doubtful again!

Then Hoopes asked if Dr. Moreland would kindly give him some information.

Moreland agreed, with his usual cadaverous politeness. Always to me an arresting and disquieting figure, this afternoon he was extraordinarily so, with his queer bleached distinction. I noted afresh his odd-looking, orange-colored eyes, one of them with a dark splash on the iris that gave them a singular expression. When he met your own eyes, which was seldom, his regard had a hard directness that affected you as if he had worn it for a screen. You found yourself blinking a little, as if to clear away some obstruction of your own vision—after which exercise you somehow expect-ed Moreland's eyes to look different. But they never did.

In answer to Hoopes' question, he stated, jingling his keys again, that he had been absent from home the whole of the evening before, from half-past seven o'clock on. He had returned home sometime after ten, he said.

"And what were you doing all that time, Dr. Moreland?"

"I was driving. As you may remember, the evening was superb. With a moon."

"I should like," said Hoopes, "to know *where* you drove."

Moreland took counsel with himself, perceptibly. Then, making up his mind (as it seemed to me) that he had better surrender his secret than make himself an object of unpleasant suspicion, he answered: "I drove to Burnsville. I very often take that drive. I think you will find that I have often been seen to take it."

Professor Ames leaned forward. "I've been attending a scientific con-vention, on the other side of Burnsville, Dr. Moreland. I passed through there last night, in my car. How many miles do you call it to Burnsville, and how long does it take?"

Moreland looked surprised at Ames' intrusion into the conversation, but he answered civilly. "It is a matter of forty miles. I do it in something close to an hour."

"And that is what you did last night?"

Moreland inclined his head. "That is what I did last night."

"I have to inform you, Dr. Moreland," said Ames, "that the road-gang started work on the Burnsville road yesterday afternoon. The road is closed, the bridge is down, and the detour by way of Black River is seventy miles. I found that out last night myself."

Moreland did not even blink. It seemed to me that his eyes dilated ever so little, for a half-second of time, but that was the only sign he gave of disturbance. "You are right, Professor Ames," he said urbanely. "Absolute-ly right. It just shows the force of habit! I am so accustomed to using the other road! But as a matter of fact, I remember now that last night I did go by Black River. In fact"—the man became positively animated—"the extra distance made me late for a professional engagement I had to see one of the doctors at the hospital. So late that when I discovered the hour, I didn't even call there. I just turned round, and came home."

"Clever devil!" I thought. "It's the next best thing to an alibi—if he needs one. He can call on Shad and me to testify to those Tuesday evening engagements."

Hoopes' next question was fairly shot at him. "Did you, either coming or going, happen to stop at Handsome Creek?"

Moreland smiled pleasantly. "To drive a hundred and forty miles, and to stop at Handsome Creek also," said Moreland, "would have taken more time than I had last night. Even with my fast car."

The honors were fairly with the doctor. Hoopes thanked him and Diana for their information, asked if he might take the road-map away with him (I thought him quite capable of looking for invisible ink), and seemed ready to depart.

But now the professor, with sudden childlike interest, requested to be shown over Moreland's laboratory. And Moreland, apparently out of pure surprise, consented. We all walked out to the shedlike building beside the river which was the doctor's own domain.

It was a strange, dim, makeshift place, long and narrow, with the door at one end. Inside, it was full of rather pathetic reminders of Moreland's professional past: his old bacteriological equipment—incubator, Petri dishes, reagents—and an ancient projector he had used in the lecture-room for showing slides. A sink with running water was beneath the one window; the shelf beside it seemed to be Moreland's only desk. A pile of manuscript in a fine irregular hand was heaped on one side. "There was a time," said the doctor, with restrained and courtly bitterness, "when I did things. Now I write about them."

Ames strolled with me a little way from the others. At the far end of the laboratory were shelves of chemicals, over which he ran his eye. "Copper sulphate—he was once interested in the chemistry of the blood, he tells me. He has all the usual things. The acids. The potassium salts. Quite complete. And of course you noticed that all of his equipment is in order, as if he were going to work again tomorrow." He looked round. "The workshop of a man of unconquerable will, who refuses to give up, and admit that life's over. Who fights to the last ditch. And isn't it to the credit of our human nature that always we salute that quality, no matter in what inexplicable combinations it is found?" His hand sketched a salute to Moreland's unused shelves. He thanked the doctor, and apologized for taking up his time; bowed farewell to Diana, and with a wiry old hand on Hoopes' elbow, steered him firmly out of the door.

Shad and I remained behind, and my cousin said, rather convention-
ally, I thought: "Sorry you've been annoyed, Moreland. Hoopes is an ass.
I apologize for ever bringing him into the neighborhood. I shall send him
off at once."

"I shouldn't do that if I were you." Moreland answered. "Better let him
rave. You don't want people to think you are trying to hush something up,
do you?" The doctor's flawless acid urbanity just kept his tone from being
insulting.

"What do you mean?"

"Merely that my own taste is all for freedom of investigation." Moreland had recovered his usual rapid flow of speech, his mirthless smile. "I
may be prejudiced by the fact that Mr. Hoopes' researches have not been
wholly barren of result: my wife has recovered a valuable jewel."

Diana said, "Shadwell has something on his mind more important than
jewels, Richard. He has—an old friend's death."

"If you had led my life," said Moreland to Shad (but he was really
speaking to his wife, though he did not look at her or address her) "you'd
think very little of death. You'd have seen too many suffering wretches to
whom death looked like a bright open door on a dark night—you'd have
compassionately helped too many of them to get there a little quicker. It's
life, my dear fellow, that's the problem; death is nothing but the answer.
And hardly an exciting one."

Shad said to me gloomily as we went out: "Cantankerous brute! He's
not very anxious to die himself, I've noticed. But he's right about Hoopes. I
can't afford to fire him. Not yet."

But on our rejoining our companions, when Hoopes said he wished to
re-examine Georgia, Shadwell exploded. He said: "Mr. Hoopes, you can't
examine a yellow dog in my house unless you improve your manners. I all
but knocked you down when you were talking to Mrs. Moreland."

"And then decided it was her husband's business, didn't you, Mr.
Dunn?" said Hoopes, with unexpected acuteness. "I could see how you felt,
but, Lord, I was handling her with gloves!"

Shad gave a groan that in spite of himself was half a laugh. The fellow
actually meant what he said. And after all, it had been Moreland's business.

Besides Georgia, Cousin Lydia's own maid was examined again. This
woman had been busy with some task in the small sitting-room that ad-
joined Cousin Lydia's room, from the windows of which, by daylight, the

course of the drive through the grounds could be seen almost all the way to the gate. Finding her eyes growing tired, she had put out the electric lamp, to rest them, and had then realized that the night outside, under the moon, was almost as bright as day. For some time she had stood at the window there, in the dark, enjoying the quiet, and was sure that for half an hour at least no car—not even a furtive car running stealthily without headlights—could have come up the drive without her seeing it plainly. More than this she could not say. The gate itself was out of her sight, behind trees; so was the spot where Georgia had seen the famous ball of fire, as well as the whole western end of the grounds, towards the quarry. The only car she had seen was "Mr. Freddy's," after a while; she had heard his voice in it, and Miss Ann Page's, and Mrs. Wing's, laughing, going round the end of the house, towards the south front. The next thing she had heard was running feet in the corridor downstairs, and her own name called, and there was Mr. Shad bringing poor Miss Lydia upstairs.

So for the time we were left where we started. Voorhees had apparently been expecting—or apprehending—a visit from someone. It might have been the unscrupulous nameless person whom Allison had heard him denouncing. It might have been Moreland, insane with jealousy. It might even have been Diana. But no one, man or woman, had been actually seen to approach the house, either on foot or by motor. The coroner's jury returned a verdict of murder by a person or persons unknown.

But when we got back to Handsome Creek that day, the verdict of the coroner's jury was still in the future.

I did not follow the general drift of the others towards the billiard-room, I strolled moodily out across the grass.

Soon Gertrude joined me, and slipped her hand through my arm. She had come determined to talk nonsense and cheer me up. "Darling, our cousin Lydia is just one more example of the fickleness of woman! Mr. Voorhees is forgotten; she has discovered an even more perfect listener in Professor Ames. He's drinking her words. It's too sweet."

"Just what is she handing out to him?" I said grumpily.

"The whole story of her last talk with Mr. Voorhees, of course. Every item. Nothing too large and nothing too small. How he loved to whittle, how he traveled with our county paper in his pocket, how he had no family of his own, how he adored onion soup. Next, the more personal touch: how nice he was, how sympathetic he was, how thrilled he was about the hex. The professor quite pricked up his ears about that, and then she was off! Professor Ames has followed the Sloap family to the quarry, to the poorhouse, to the graveyard. He has also learned how many prizes Shad took at school, and how far the bones stuck out of his arm when it was broken. When the recital got too bloody, I slipped out." She patted my arm. "Come! there are tea and highballs in the billiard-room."

Afternoon tea that day was a silent function. A great heap of telegrams at Shadwell's side (they had been pouring in since morning) showed that Voorhees had been a man of many friendships. But he had had no close family ties; he was a widower, and childless. A cablegram from his only sister, living in Florence, begged that Shadwell would arrange for cremation. It was settled that Allison, Professor Ames, and I should accompany him the next day to Washington, on that depressing errand; a group of Voorhees' associates and friends from the North would meet us there. Freddy was to be left in charge at Handsome Creek, and we should be back by bedtime.

After tea, the professor disappeared from the house, and Allison, with whom he had arranged to drive down to the village, couldn't find him. So Gertrude and he and I set out as a search party. We found Ames down by the creek, sitting uncomfortably on a stone wall which was not quite low enough for him, so that he steadied himself precariously by digging the back of his heels into a crack.

"I have temporarily discarded the methods of the laboratory," he said rather forlornly. He looked like a little boy whose balloon has burst. "I find I've got a *feeling* about how things happened here last night!" He might have been confessing that he found he had leprosy or bubonic plague. His eyes pleaded for understanding and pity. "I can't shake it off."

"Why do you want to shake it off, sir?" said Allison. "Everything helps;

"Because it's a very unpleasant feeling. I feel that I've discovered certain important indications bearing upon the murder of Mr. Voorhees. And yet they lead to an irrational conclusion. It's unscientific, it doesn't make sense."

"Put it up to Shadwell, anyway," I said.

"Mr. Dunn would laugh at it. But I can't get rid of it, I simply can't!"

"If it's unscientific," said Gertrude mischievously, "I can't imagine you entertaining it for five seconds yourself!"

He shook his head at her in an absent way. "My dear lady, I've watched a bird get a 'feeling.' How does the young female of the oriole, in her first mating season, know that the eggs, which she does not yet know she is going to lay, should be laid in a horsehair nest? But she does know. She sees straws and sticks and clay all around her, she sees other birds building nests of them—that's all right with her, the idea just doesn't interest her, somehow. But presently she spies a horsehair, and (presumably) a little bell rings inside her, and she says, '*There* it is!'" He looked up with sudden seriousness at Gertrude. "Well, my dear, I've spied my horsehair!"

CHAPTER IX

The professor and Allison returned from the village in company with Hoopes, who had some news: he had discovered that Voorhees had eaten his last dinner at a little hotel near the courthouse.

There had been nothing furtive about it. Nor had he had the air of expecting anyone. "That doesn't prove that he wasn't, of course," said Hoopes. "But neither does the character of the place prove that if he did, the person he expected was shady. It's the only hotel in Frisbie. Low characters and bootleggers go there, but so do the lawyers and the witnesses when court is sitting. They have to. There is nowhere else to go, except lunch-counters. I should say it was quite respectable. He might even have been expecting a lady," said Hoopes, with an air of defiance. He looked at Ames; it was evident that already they had disagreed.

Ames bristled, and said belligerently: "Mr. Hoopes, I have already expressed my opinion that to inquire up and down the main street, as you've been doing, whether Mr. Voorhees had been seen in company of a lady, was unworthy of the intelligence of a six-year-old child. Especially after you had been at some pains to impress on Mrs. Moreland's servant the fact that you had suspicions of the doctor.—If you say that this is purely destructive criticism, and therefore unhelpful, I will give you a constructive suggestion: it will pay you totally to readjust your theory of the crime. There was no burst of animosity; this was not a murder in hot blood. It was the cool work of a man to whom human life isn't particularly sacred. In other words, not a passionate deed. A callous one."

"Don't you think, Professor Ames," said Shadwell, in a regretful and somber voice, "that you are really supporting what is evidently Mr. Hoopes' theory? Aren't you describing the sort of man whose view of human life is the one that Moreland expressed this morning?"

"I should certainly not like to have Dr. Moreland for an enemy," said Ames, but you must not put words into my mouth, Mr. Dunn. I'm merely saying that in our criminal I am convinced I see a person who has done murder before."

You're wrong, professor," said Hoopes, politely enough, but dogmatically. "This is an amateur's crime."

"I agree with you. But we may not mean the same thing by the word, 'amateur.'"

"I mean something that would fit both Dr. and Mrs. Moreland, as well as just about everybody in this house!"

Shadwell opened his lips and closed them again. But I said: "Then you'd better start giving the third degree to Miss Perryman and Mr. Dunn and me. We were the three left at home."

Hoopes looked at me almost pityingly. "Do you think I haven't considered that, Mr. Wing? If it weren't for the monkey-business with the lights, which makes it plain that the gentleman was looking for somebody from outside, why, I might have considered the possibility of an inside job. But as it is, you people in the house seem to be eliminated." He looked rather sorry. "Besides, this was a one-man job, and all of you have all your time accounted for while the murder was being done."

Cousin Lydia said crisply: "Excuse me. My time isn't accounted for! Aren't you perhaps forgetting that I was the first person known to have gone into the library after the last moment when we can be certain Mr. Voorhees was alive?"

"Or that I was the last person known to have seen him in life?" said Shad relentlessly. "For when Georgia saw him, he must have been already dead."

Hoopes ignored Shadwell's irony, but he thought Cousin Lydia's worth an answer. "No, ma'am. I hadn't forgotten. Your case is different from the others: you could have killed him, and said you found him that way. But that's where psychology comes in," he explained kindly. "You're not the type."

My cousin Lydia for once was speechless. And Shadwell looked at the psychologist with quite a new expression. "Mr. Hoopes," he said, with sardonic amusement, "no matter how many murders are committed at Handsome Creek, as long as I'm alive you get the job of unraveling them. I apologize for my criticism."

"No offense, Mr. Dunn. People aren't hardly themselves with their first murder in the house. The next one you won't take so hard."

"You encourage me," said Shad dryly. "But none of this explains your insinuations against Mrs. Moreland!"

"Look at the facts, Mr. Dunn. We find a small article of Mrs. Moreland's, valuable in itself, and also of sentimental interest maybe, in very close and unexplained proximity to the effects of the murdered man. Miss Avery, being her good friend, telephones Mrs. Moreland. (Oh, I don't blame her. It was quite the sporting thing to do.) Well, the lady, being, as Dr. Ames correctly noted, as quick a thinker as Miss Avery herself, thought of a very smart question to ask: Was the miniature found in the frame? Now don't you see where that lands us?"

"It was a perfectly natural question!" said Ann Page.

"No, Miss Avery, natural is just what it wasn't, if she really believed the frame to have been lost or stolen. For in that case she would have expected the picture to be taken out and destroyed at once. Fear of identification. But if she had given it away, then her question was clever. She expected the miniature to be there, of course, but wanted to pretend that she didn't."

"But if all that is so," said Cousin Lydia, "where is the miniature?"

"Madam," said Hoopes lugubriously, "I wish to the Lord I knew."

It was impossible not to laugh at his tone.

"But if you're suspecting Dr. Moreland of the murder," said Ames plaintively, "isn't the technique in that case too crude, too casual? From all indications of the type of mind involved, and from every personal characteristic of the doctor himself, we ought logically, if he is guilty, to find ourselves up against a perfect alibi. And he hasn't a sign of one."

"What do you mean by the type of mind involved?"

"This crime was carefully premeditated, by a murderer of unusually brilliant parts. In fact, as a criminal he seems to me almost a genius."

"He's got *me* guessing, if you mean that," said Hoopes, with perfect seriousness.

"He is the man I heard Mr. Voorhees quarreling with," said Allison stubbornly. "Don't forget that Mr. Voorhees really was robbed of a hundred dollars! Is it your theory, Mr. Hoopes, that Dr. Moreland killed Mr. Voorhees with the idea of securing a sum of money to indemnify himself for the disappearance of his wife's picture? Or what?"

Hoopes kept his air of regretful candor. "That hundred-dollar bill, Mr. Allison—that really is a poser. But certainly no ordinary burglar takes one bill, and leaves a lot of others, now, does he?"

"And it didn't seem to have been just dropped," I said. "It was all crushed together in a wad, as if intended to be—well, thrown at somebody! My guess is that Voorhees was paying blackmail, and tried to get out of it too cheap this time; the chap got mad, threw the money back at him, and knifed him. But still that doesn't account for the diamond frame."

"Let's leave the diamonds out of it for a minute," said Freddy. "Here's what seems funny to me; Mr. Voorhees evidently had an appointment to call up this unknown double-crosser. The hornet-sting was just a pretext to get away from the river. But he left—there's the point—in a perfectly good humor. He had been larking and laughing and perspiring and trying to tear Shad's clothes off of him and generally raising Cain in a temperature of ninety-five degrees; he was in a state of hilarity that wouldn't have been natural at all in a man who had been disgustingly double-crossed by somebody and was in a rage about it. In this mood, on his way home, he calls at Diana's. Calls, by the way, in what must have been extraordinary haste, for he stopped just as he was, hot and rumpled and filthy—I assure you his shirt was pasted to his back when I saw him, he and Shad had made themselves look like two toughs. Well—he misses Diana, leaves a common Standard Oil road-map for her—of all things!—and dashes home and changes his clothes, all before he has had any converse at all with the man that Allison heard him abusing over the telephone. And what I want to know is: Why did he change *then?*"

"Say, that about changing his clothes is a good point!" said Hoopes, with revived animation. "How did he know already that he'd be eating dinner away from home?"

"Do we have to be so subtle?" asked Allison impatiently. "Can't a man change just because he's dirty and hot? Here's how it looks to me: the ugly news about the crooked deal, whatever it was, didn't break till he got to the telephone, and it gave him a shock. I think he just decided to eat his dinner alone, and think things over—he wasn't up to a social hour at Handsome

Creek. Besides, he had his plans to make, before his appointment to talk with the fellow; you remember he said, 'I'm leaving at once'?"

"Yes," said Hoopes, "and that's another nut to crack. Where did he have to rush away to, so fast, as soon as he heard the news? What was the business that needed attention right off? Why should this scrap change his schedule?"

Shad said, with his grimmest expression, "None of it makes sense."

"Well, here is something that does! Suppose that telephone-talk didn't refer to business matters at all?"

"What did it refer to, then?" asked Allison.

"To the lovely Mrs. Moreland, and her unhappy marriage! Isn't her unhappiness 'quite transparent'? Hasn't she stuck to her husband in spite of a situation that is certainly 'all wet'? We don't know yet just how badly Dr. Moreland has taken advantage of her loyalty, but he looks to me like a man who would go pretty far, and Mrs. Moreland had plenty of chances to tell Mr. Voorhees her side of it. Does it occur to you that on Tuesday afternoon she may even have passed a letter into his hand in the boat? He makes an excuse to get away from Mr. Dunn, and read it; he is upset by it, and calls up the doctor to make a date to talk it over. And if he had fallen for the lady himself, he might have promised to leave at once because he was acting disinterestedly, and didn't want to make trouble for her."

"Do you mean he'd have fallen that hard in twenty-four hours?" I asked incredulously.

"Well, he had known her a little, before. How do you know he didn't come down here on her account, really?—And now listen to what I got from the telephone girl; it clicks with the Moreland end of it. She says she was so mad with her girl friend when those calls were being made that she doesn't think she'd even have remembered calling Handsome Creek if the number hadn't been hard to get. That impressed it on her mind. So maybe the other number wasn't unfamiliar to her, as we've assumed—maybe it just slipped her memory because it was easy to get! And what does that call to my mind? Why, the picture of Dr. Moreland, at just about twenty minutes past six, by what the maid said, sipping milk in a big chair with a telephone not a foot from his hand!"

He was interrupted by a cry from Cousin Lydia. "Look at Professor Ames!—Shadwell, the professor isn't well!"

Ames certainly presented a strange appearance, he had almost the look of a man in a trance. He sat limp in his chair, his lips parted, with every trace of expression wiped from his face. He breathed hard, and he was pale. But he pulled himself together, the next minute, and declared he felt perfectly fit.

Cousin Lydia refused to accept his assurances of good health. He must "have something." She rang the bell. And it was Robinson who answered it.

Ames looked up. "Catch, Robinson!" he said, a little feebly. Something brightly metallic went spinning over and over through the air; it seemed heavy, from the apparent weight of the impact on the negro's palm.

"My brand-new automatic," said Ames, with a faint complacency, to Cousin Lydia. "I bought it—with some difficulty—this afternoon. But I have just decided that I am not going to need it tonight."

CHAPTER X

When I got back to Handsome Creek on Thursday evening with Shadwell and the others, from our dismal journey to Washington, it speedily became apparent to me that if any detail of the family history had not been imparted to Professor Ames before we left, Cousin Lydia was now prepared to make good that omission. His information about the Dunns and Averys was well on the way to become as encyclopaedic as her own.

Nor did her confidences weary the professor. He seemed ready to listen by the hour. There was one result before bedtime that same evening: he stepped on Shadwell's toes in a somewhat unfortunate manner. "Miss Perryman tells me, Mr. Dunn," he said to my cousin, "that most of the beautiful old furniture here, and the fine portraits, came to you, with a fortune besides, from an uncle."

"Yes. He was a very prosperous old bachelor, and had accumulated a lot of family things. He died shortly after my return."

At this point my wife compressed her lips ever so slightly. She never could help compressing them when the family relics were mentioned. Up to the time of Shad's triumphant return, rich and successful, to restore the glories of Handsome Creek, the will of our old bachelor relative had been understood to provide for the equitable distribution of these treasures among the various nephews, nieces, and cousins. But the imagination of the failing and purblind old gentleman had been fired by Shad's odyssey, and in a burst of enthusiasm he had made Shad, to all intents and purposes, his sole heir. Small legacies of money did indeed fall to the rest of us, but Shad got the bulk of the money and all the furniture and other treasures, including the ancestral snuffbox that had been a present from Lafayette. Still, the fault—if fault you could call it—wasn't Shad's. He had

barely known his uncle, and had certainly never tried to be made his resid-
uary legatee. There was really no hard feeling on anybody's part.

Gertrude couldn't resist taking one small dig at him, though. "I remember poor Mr. Voorhees' saying, professor," she said, "that if he had been in
the family's shoes, he wouldn't have cared about the money, but he'd have
wanted to fight for the snuffbox."

"The family," said my cousin, "realizes that as I am a bachelor too, and
unlikely to marry, the stuff will get divided in due course."

"But isn't it almost your duty to marry," said Ames, with benignity, "if
only to explode the superstition about Handsome Creek? Of course you
yourself do own the place, but—"

"But I had to buy it from the creditors, is that what you mean? You are
quite correct. My uncle's estate I did inherit, but not my father's house."
My cousin had the haughty look he always had when anyone suggested
that he should pay the slightest attention to the old saga of the Sloaps,
except as an amusement for his great-aunt Lydia. "But even so—notwith-
standing the temptation to make a monkey out of the famous hex—I am
not a marrying man."

He was so positive and so curt, and he left us so abruptly, that I should
have felt sorry for the small professor, had it not been clear that both tone
and manner went completely over his head.

Ames only blinked amiably after Shad's retreating form. "In other
words, Mr. Dunn has not yet met the lady!"

"If only he *could* meet 'the lady,' Professor Ames!" Cousin Lydia sighed.
"Once or twice I have thought I saw signs in him of getting what old-fashioned people used to call 'broody,' and have hoped he was becoming interested in someone—but it always wore off."

"'Broody,'" repeated Gertrude. "It's a perfect word. It absolutely de-
scribes the state of my poor Freddy! I wish Ann Page would accept him,
and be done with it. He moons around, and goggles at her in the most
half-witted way—simply pitiful! Why is it a man cannot be in love, and still
look, in the presence of his idol, as if he had an atom of sense?—Here they
come now. Look at him!"

Freddy did indeed wear the typical expression, at once groveling and
blissful, of the tolerated but not yet accepted lover. I judged, however,
that the end of his suspense was near. There was a tremulous sweetness
about Ann Page that was very touching. I had a sudden tender memory

of Gertrude looking very much that same way; I smiled a little at her, and discovered that she was smiling a little at me— Yes, I quite pitied Shadwell for having no love-affair.

But I was successfully diverted from such sentimental thoughts, by what happened later that evening. Strolling up to bed rather tardily, with Freddy, Gertrude and I paused before his bedroom door. On the second bed sat Ames, whom we had believed asleep long ago. He appeared lost in unpalatable thought, his hair was sticking up as if a gale had passed through it. He had sat down, and simply forgotten to undress. He looked as if he had sat there for hours.

"Something about the way you look, professor," said Freddy, with a manner that was more serious than his words, "tells me it is not for nought that every single hair of your head is standing on end! I believe you've thought of something. You've got a lead. A clue."

"I've got more than a clue," said Ames dryly. "I've got an infernal scientific certainty."

"You don't mean it!" Freddy cried.

"I know why a murder should logically have been committed at Handsome Creek."

"Gosh!"

"I've known for almost twenty-four hours—I mean I have known theoretically—in what direction to look for the slayer of our poor friend. The extraordinary motive is clear to me, and why it had to be done in just this way. Not a flaw in the reasoning! The whole sequence of events leading up to the murder is beautifully satisfying to the mind."

"You do not look to me," said Gertrude, "as if your mind were beautifully satisfied."

"Oh, there's a hitch," said Ames. "One single hitch. But it's enough. The person who by all the laws of logic should have committed the murder, didn't do it!"

"Then who did?"

"Somebody else, of course," said Ames forlornly, rumpling up his hair.

That sent us to bed both tantalized and discouraged. But Gertrude, being a woman, was able to turn from the depressing subject to one of a more romantic kind, She woke me out of my first nap by saying in a sleepy but thoughtful voice, "Carty, Cousin Lydia has given me a notion: Shadwell was a lot too emphatic this afternoon about that marrying business."

"For Pete's sake, did you wake me up to say that?"

"Shad isn't himself. And it isn't all on account of the murder, either. I've been thinking of what you said about his getting so mad with Mr. Hoopes at Elmington. You mark my words, Shad's going 'broody' over Diana Moreland!"

"Oh, go to sleep!" I said. "What if he is?"

But whatever may have been the private heartaches of Shadwell or of any of us, the mystery still surrounding the death of poor Voorhees had by Friday morning got on all our nerves. Gertrude bit my head off a dozen times before breakfast. And the state of Professor Ames, taking his morning coffee, was even worse; he was hollow-eyed, fidgety, and snappish. He was the picture of a man whose cares had spoiled his sleep.

About eleven o'clock Gertrude and Ann Page were on their way downstairs in my company when something happened that showed how people in our condition can fly to pieces. The slight cause was out of all proportion to the devastating effects; it was nothing more serious than the sudden rattling sharp cascade of a lot of wooden checkers on the hardwood floor of the hall. But it might have been a machine-gun going off, from the way the girls screamed.

"Oooo-*ooh!*" shrieked Gertrude, clutching my arm. And "*Eeee*-eeh!" squealed Ann Page. The maddening rat-tat-tat-tat of the checkers as they hopped and rolled and skipped and tapped seemed as if it would never stop—I was ready to scream myself. And little Ames, standing in the hall among the jittering devilish things, looked ripe for mayhem. He called to the girls, less savagely than I should have done in his place, but crossly enough, "There, there, there, for God's sake! The young man did it by accident."

We saw an overwhelmed and apologetic electrician in overalls peering out of the cupboard where the games were. He had knocked a stack of them down, and the shrieks from above had quite demoralized him. He said: "I'm surely sorry, miss—ma'am. Those things didn't used to be kept in here, or I'd have looked out for 'em. I'm awful sorry." In his embarrassment he dropped a handful of fuses with a still louder rattle, and Gertrude screamed again; she was by that time in such a state that actually tears had been shaken out of her.

It was a madhouse scene. The poor young man plunged his head and shoulders into the cupboard again, and did not reappear, though a sort of litany of remorse and apology continued to come out. The crowning touch of unreason was supplied when Ames, who had been trying to block the hopping, rolling little black-and-red disks as they streamed toward him, suddenly gave a kick to the nearest one, seized his hat, ran out of the hall-door, and was seen no more.

When he turned up again, two hours later, he was hot and apparently tired, but a different man. To Gertrude and Ann Page he apologized meekly for his bad temper. "My dears, you must forgive an old fellow! I could never hope to make you understand what happened to my mental processes there in the hall! Gertrude, will you promise to come to me and scream loudly in my ear whenever my brain declines to function? The effect is miraculous."

"Professor, darling, even your insults are intriguing!" The dear girl, thank Heaven, is easily mollified. ("Not realizing at the time, you wretch," she told him afterwards, "what a fool you were making of me.—My screams, indeed!")

That afternoon, when we were sitting in on one of Shadwell's consultations with Hoopes, the professor bobbed up vigorously, so to speak, in a brand-new place.

Looking back, as I do now, on the experiences of that memorable week, I can see with what extraordinary craft, from day to day, Ames led us along. He kept the secret of that "feeling" he had spoken of; he even joked about his mysterious one-hundred-to-one shot. He fed his idea to us—his horrifying idea of our actual situation at Handsome Creek—bit by bit. He told us nothing that mattered until he had prepared us, though only subconsciously perhaps, to hear it. Only step by step—and with more than one halt in his progress, because he himself had lost the path—did he reveal to us the way that he had traveled to reach his conclusion, and that we were so shudderingly to tread behind him.

He began on this occasion by saying, "Mr. Dunn, I've a reason to ask myself whether our murderer, far from being a person of breeding and education (as in the theory of our friend Mr. Hoopes), may not be from the very lowest classes."

Shadwell looked skeptical. "That telephone conversation sounded as if Voorhees knew him pretty intimately."

"If so, it is necessary to assume (necessary to my own theory, I mean) that our criminal has risen far above his original station, for Voorhees could hardly have known him otherwise. Was not Mr. Voorhees quite as well born as you are, Mr. Dunn? You went to the same school and had the same associates, did you not?"

"Why, certainly," said Shad.

"And he really does not seem to have had—in his own class—a personal enemy in the world. All his friends, when I talked to them in Washington, agreed with me there. He was singularly amiable and philanthropic."

"You conclude, then," said Shad, looking puzzled, "that no possibility is left but the underworld? The professional crook?"

"Oh, not necessarily a professional! Merely a person without the usual standards. For, I repeat, this strikes me as a very cool and calculated murder. And I believe it to have been done, oddly enough, without personal ill-will!"

I said: "But, professor, it was certainly impulsive. He used Voorhees' own knife."

"How do we know," argued Freddy, "that he did not come provided with half a dozen assorted knives in his pocket? His using Voorhees' knife may just show his presence of mind. He was smart enough to see the advantage of picking up a chance weapon that he could leave behind him."

"Your inferences are in part correct," said Ames.

Hoopes said unsympathetically, "No doubt Professor Ames has some private dope that the rest of us are not acquainted with."

"I have no private data of any kind, except those that have been open to us all. Nothing that's inaccessible to anybody in this room. The only thing I possess at this moment that is not shared by all of you is something that I have worked out for myself: an hypothesis."

"Worked out from exactly the same start that we've all got?" asked Freddy, as if he could not believe his ears.

Ames nodded. He went on: "The murderer of my present hypothesis is a dangerous and ruthless man in the prime of life. Certain indications make me place his age at thirty-five or six. He is practically uneducated. He had, I imagine, not much schooling at any age, and none at all after he was—let us say—fifteen."

"But, professor," cried Cousin Lydia, seeing an opening for her favorite subject, "a boy can be very well educated at that age! Shadwell took four prizes at the Chalmers School the year he was fifteen. At sixteen he took the mathematics medal, and at seventeen—when he ran away—he was equal to any college sophomore—"

"My dear Miss Perryman," protested Ames, "I am talking about the sort of human being who never saw the inside of a decent school."

"Well, I don't see what evidence you think you've got," said Hoopes sulkily.

"I regret to say, I have nothing yet that could be produced in a court of law. I shouldn't know what to do with our murderer, even supposing we had him here in the room with handcuffs on him. I warn you, the actual case against him is all to be constructed! We have a dead body, but no connection that's susceptible of proof between that dead body and any person living. We are dealing, as I have said before, with a very uncommon criminal."

The professor was in deadly earnest. So much so that I date from that hour the beginnings of my own serious personal uneasiness. He continued: "I can imagine a certain kind of research into crime that would be like deducing the completed skeleton from a single fossil bone. But the next step in my own speculations isn't so scientific as that.—Having as yet unearthed no tangible reason why the man of my hypothesis should have wished to kill Mr. Voorhees, I am driven to look farther.—Mr. Dunn, I've been talking to your postmaster, a remarkably intelligent fellow," said Ames, with the candid and unsophisticated and confiding expression that already I was learning to distrust. "And he told me an interesting and suggestive thing. He says that all your colored people are convinced that your family hex of so many years ago and its more or less uncanny sequels are at the bottom of your troubles here. Should you say they could possibly have anything to go on?"

Shad colored irritably. "They have an ungodly amount of imagination to go on, at all times. But my own powers of credulity stop at witchcraft."

"Oh, I don't refer to anything supernatural. But there is often something not quite scientifically explicable about the perceptions of the primitive races that we are pleased to consider inferior."

Hoopes said, "Golly, can't we stick to real life?"

It seemed a good suggestion to me. As for Gertrude, she murmured to me: "The professor knows that he can make Shad indignantly deny that the earth is round, merely by suggesting that the colored people believe it. But why waste time? Shad already disbelieves in the hex!"

"If you wish to discuss more material things, Mr. Hoopes, very well!" said Ames. I assure you it comes to the same thing in the end. Let us talk about a subject that's material and real enough for anyone. I refer to Mr. Shadwell Dunn's flannel trousers!—I understand, Mr. Dunn, that the trousers Mr. Voorhees wore on Tuesday afternoon were yours? And that he had to roll them up?"

Shad, by this time apparently past astonishment, just nodded.

"It is also true, Miss Lydia tells me, that the difference in your stature was all in the legs. Your height was the same when you sat down. And both of your heads were black.—Has it occurred to you that the murderer of Mr. Voorhees, who came up on him from behind, might have killed him by mistake for *you?*"

As it happened, when he spoke I was turned towards Shadwell, and I saw the alteration in him. I thought at the moment, and I still think today, that no more authentic look of pure stupefaction ever blotted from human face all other expression. For a moment he was stunned. And then, deep down in Shadwell, amazement at the suggestion gave way to something else, an emotion instantaneous, obscure, and powerful, that he did not want to betray. And he succeeded in suppressing any sign of its nature; it might have been anger, terror, relief, humiliation it might have been anything at all. His features locked themselves up over it. Now that I understand all the turmoil of his unprepared thoughts then—what deep-lying emotions must have surged up in him, and with what an overpowering shock of surprise the suggestion came I am even more astonished, in retrospect than I was at the time, by his power of self-command. Only his blood he could not control, and it rose in a dark excited flood to his throat, to his cheeks, to his forehead and his very ears. He said with exaggerated force, "That's inconceivable!"

"You are so sure that you have no enemies, Mr. Dunn?"

"Good Lord, no! Far from it. Do I look like the sort of spineless creature that never made one? But I can truly say that if I have a single enemy nearer to me tonight than—say—ten thousand miles, I don't know it. Why on earth should your friend the ex-convict, or whatever else you believe him to be—the man from the slums that you've described to us—want to murder me?"

"I've said nothing about slums, you have misunderstood me," said Ames.

"Maybe so," said Shad. "But still I'm afraid, professor, that what poor Voorhees got was meant for him, and nobody else."

"And yet," said Ames, with his vaguest, most innocent expression, "nobody ever cursed Mr. Voorhees."

Freddy, taken off his guard, gave an unfortunate little snort of amusement. Shad looked that way for a minute, and his face darkened, he almost scowled.

The professor rambled on: "Oh, I'm not asking you to go in for vulgar superstition! But has there ever been current among the negroes, to your knowledge, any rumor that the unhappy lad who fell into the quarry did not die of his fall?"

"Since the unfortunate little devil," said Shad grimly, "was found with his head under water in the pool in which he had been lying all night, there's little doubt that life was extinct. But perhaps his soul goes marching on! Perhaps the restless ghost or the resurrected body of Thomas Jefferson Sloap may have come back and planted a knife between Voorhees' shoulder-blades, by mistake for me! But the question still remains: If a man-killing, revivified corpse rose out of the grave to murder me, why last night? Why not earlier—any time in the last three years? Why not later—any time in the next three?"

"Yes—why indeed?" murmured Ames in a mortified tone.

Shadwell laughed, not very pleasantly. "Your hypothesis is interesting, Professor Ames. Of course an unknown mysterious enemy may be on my trail. How do I know? The mere fact that I can't remember any enemies among the dregs of the population doesn't prove that I haven't any. But this is the twentieth century, and witchcraft is out. Forget the hex. You'll have to look elsewhere."

"Then it is you and I against Mr. Hoopes. He already is looking elsewhere!" said Ames flatly. His tone was warning, almost ominous. "And you know in what direction."

Shad laughed again. "At least he doesn't suggest that Moreland is after *me!*"

CHAPTER XI

That evening, Shadwell, himself, was driving Hoopes down to the village. On the way they were to stop at Elmington. Shadwell had directed Hoopes to give back the much-discussed road-map to Diana, and apparently was going along to see that he did it.

Hoopes had made one more contribution to our theories about the still unidentified "ball of fire." "I think that fellow drove in without lights," he said, "and drove out the same way. His slip was that just from force of habit he turned his lights on as he started his engine. He switched them right off again, of course, and just prayed that nobody saw them.—I'm still working on that. Following it up."

And just before they were to go, Shadwell came to me. "Carty, Hoopes has asked to have a talk with me away from Professor Ames. And I'd like you to be present."

Hoopes wanted to say that he was not working on what he called "the Moreland line" alone; he had still other ideas. "I'm working on the telephone talk from a brand-new angle.—How do we know that this young Allison ever heard Mr. Voorhees talking on the telephone at all?"

Shadwell looked at him as if he had been a noxious insect. "You are under no obligation to take my word about my part of it, Mr. Hoopes, verified as it is only by my own servant. But I think you'll find that when I say I talked to Mr. Voorhees over the telephone on Tuesday afternoon, and that he used just the words that Allison reports, most people will believe me."

"Oh, don't get me wrong, Mr. Dunn. I believe you, because the telephone girl swears to that part of it, too." Hoopes did not seem to realize that an expression of confidence phrased in just that way might be offensive. "But what was to hinder Mr. Allison from making all the rest of it up?

We've nobody's word but his own that Mr. Voorhees ever had the other conversation." I started to speak, but he held up his hand. "Let me finish putting this before you gentlemen, please! I don't know, because nobody has told me, why Mr. Allison had to make his trip to see this old gentleman that's snooping around here now, trying to teach me my business. You've all been pretty close-mouthed about that. Oh, I've seen that you were covering something up. Of course, you don't have to tell me any more than you want to. But I've talked pretty frankly with the sheriff. If there was bad blood between Voorhees and Allison, it might have been all to the young fellow's advantage to fill you full of a story about the other man's having a quarrel with somebody else— And now, Mr. Dunn, I suppose I'm fired from this job."

"Far from it, Mr. Hoopes," said my cousin, with commendable restraint, though I saw the veins swell on his forehead. "I give you credit for sense enough to know that by talking to the sheriff you've made it necessary for me to keep you. Very neat. I can't have the whole county thinking that you were sent back to Washington because you were getting warm! So you can stay and be damned to you. But you'll keep a still tongue in your head after this till you have some proof against somebody—proof, do you hear?—or I'll break every bone in your body."

Hoopes didn't flinch. "I'd be a lot nearer to getting some real proof if you'd tell me everything you know, Mr. Dunn," he returned. "I've been thinking over some of the things that old professor said." And with a wag of his head to drive that home, he withdrew.

I don't pretend that I hadn't by this time a similar idea myself, though it was far from having any reference to Allison. Naturally I got it where I get most of my ideas: from my wife. It was after Ames had put his electrifying question to Shadwell. "Imagine poor Shad," she said to me, "if he has to choose between clearing up the mystery of his friend's death, and keeping the cover on some terrible thing in his own life! I don't mean any disgrace, of course. But it might be something horribly painful, just the same. And think of having a deadly enemy after you, and yet not daring to hand him over to justice, for fear of the truth's coming out!" So though Hoopes' dark hints about Allison seemed laughable, the shrewdness with which he had guessed Shad's lack of candor was less amusing. That my cousin was a man with a painful secret seemed to me to grow clearer hour by hour.

When Hoopes and Shadwell had at last driven off, that evening, Allison said to his guardian, "Mr. Dunn has got over his temper now. But you want to watch your step, sir. He's certainly touchy about the hex."

"Oh, dear me," said Ames plaintively, "it's fatal for people to start telling me things to avoid. I'm so absent-minded, it just acts as a suggestion. I resemble the little boy learning to bicycle, who always hits the stone in the road if he tries too hard not to!—However, I'll endeavor to remember that Mr. Dunn resents it if anyone attaches importance to the old story, is that it?"

"Not quite," I said. "He doesn't care how much importance other people attach to it—he positively eggs us on. What he resents is the slightest hint, however small, that he himself attaches any."

"Mr. Dunn prides himself on his personal courage, I know," said Ames. "Well, as I say, I'll try to remember."

That night, Cousin Lydia went up early. Ann Page and Freddy took a stroll outside. My wife and the professor gave Allison and me a sound licking at old-fashioned whist, and then we were ready for bed.

In the hall, we were joined by Freddy and Ann Page, coming in from their stroll. They reported the world drowned in mist. All of Ann Page's little rings of hair were curly with damp; her eyes were stars, her cheeks were roses. But Freddy looked depressed; Ann Page was not in a serious humor tonight. Plainly she had given him no chance to propose. We were all still chattering at the foot of the stairs when Shadwell returned, and then we stood and chattered a little while longer. Ann Page wanted to know just how Diana had looked and talked, and did she seem herself again, and didn't Shadwell think she was the loveliest thing on earth—much too good for that graven image she was married to?

Freddy said: "You're prejudiced, Ann Page. Dr. Moreland's queer, but I believe Hoopes has him wrong. And you have too. He's really an impressive sort of person. Unplumbed depths inside him. Cavernous. Extinct-volcano effect."

"Extinct?" said Gertrude. "Maybe so, maybe not. I wouldn't count on it."

"You could, darling. You could bet your immortal soul on it!" declared Ann Page. "That man's not human.—Is he, Shadwell?"

Shad was plainly restive under the questioning; he hardly did Ann Page the honor to look at her when he answered though, leaning there on the stair-rail, two or three steps above us, my little cousin was quite a lovely thing herself. I thought, "Can't she see he wishes she'd drop the subject?" And in a moment he fairly turned his back on her and walked away.

Then Gertrude said, "People, I feel as if I'd been standing in this hall for most of my life!" and started upstairs. She hissed into my ear as she passed me, "Bring the professor into our room when you come up. Don't let him get away from you."

"And now, Professor Ames," she said, as soon as the door was shut on us, "why were you trying this afternoon to get Shadwell upset? I know when you're doing things on purpose."

The professor chose the part of wisdom, which was to surrender at once. "My dear," he said, "your cousin Mr. Dunn was bound to be angry when he learned that anyone, no matter who, dares to connect the family hex with last night's tragedy. It seemed to me wise to let him work his anger off as soon as possible."

Gertrude shook her head at him. "You aren't fooling me at all. There's a lot more back of it than that! You were making him angry about the hex to distract his attention from something else that you didn't want him to put his mind on. There's something he mustn't suspect till you're quite ready to tell him—is that it?"

"My dear," said Ames, rumpling his white topknot with the air of great discomfiture, "I'm quite ashamed not to be as clever as you think I am. I only wish— Good Heavens, what's that?"

We listened. There were flying footsteps on the stair—footsteps with the beat of panic—they were at the door—Ann Page burst in, panting, with ruffled hair and distended eyes; she flung herself into Gertrude's arms. "Oh, don't let me go!—I'm so terrified!" she sobbed.

"What is it, darling? What is it? What happened?"

"An awful man—a dreadful man—"

"Where?"

"Outside in the mist, in the dark! Where I had dropped my scarf, and went down to look for it. He was prowling about in the bushes."

I jumped up. "I'll call Shad and the others!"

Ames stopped me. "Wait a minute!—What was the man like, Miss Avery?" he asked eagerly.

"I don't know, it was dark. I was stooping over. All at once—he—he—*grabbed* me—but I fought him, and twisted loose, and ran."

"But what was he like?"

She said, shuddering: "No bristles. Smooth-shaven. Yes, he got his awful face as close as that! It was just a touch, but I could feel. And he was clean—not smelly and foul—he wasn't a common tramp. But oh, such a sickening whiskey-breath!"

I took a stride towards the door, but Ames had got a grip of quite surprising strength on my sleeve. "Wait now," he said rapidly. "A whiskey-breath, my dear, means nothing unless we have the image of a ruffian in our minds. Are you sure that it wasn't a practical joke? After all, three men of the five of us in this very house have had a drink inside of the last half-hour. Mr. Dunn and myself are the only teetotalers. And if somebody thought he'd startle you for a minute—"

Ann Page interrupted him. "You don't understand. Really, it wasn't a practical joke. I'd—I'd have known. The grab didn't last but a minute, but it was *real!*"

Ames released my sleeve. "All right, then. Go!"

I dashed out, and roused the house. Allison and Freddy in pajamas, and Shadwell in shirt and trousers, toothbrush in hand, came running; in two minutes we were out in the mist, on the terrace side of the house, beating the laurel bushes along the drive, and making enough noise to inform a dozen ruffians how to keep out of our way. Freddy was like a wild man. He would hardly listen to Shadwell, who said heavily at last, "It's no use, boys." Freddy would have beat the bushes all night. We almost had to drag him with us when we went back to the house.

It was half an hour later, after I had been dismissed to Ann Page's own little white-curtained chamber, and Ann Page had been tucked into my bed to spend the night in Gertrude's company, that Gertrude followed me for a moment into my banishment. She slipped in excitedly, with her hair pulled straight back into a high tight round bathing-knot, and her lovely bare legs gleaming below the mandarin coat that was her only garment. "I was just stepping into the tub, darling, when I had a thought! I believe the professor wanted that man to get away!"

"What? A horrible slick degenerate like that?" I exclaimed.

"No, Carty, that man was the other kind! The human-mongrel sort that Professor Ames talked about. The man from the gutter who has lifted himself by his boot-straps out of the mud, and has learned to take a bath. The professor pretended he was talking about an imaginary person. A type. But

I tell you this creature is the one—he's the living man out of the unknown that's after Shad!"

"My word, woman!" I exclaimed. "Listen to sense. It's impossible for the professor or anybody else to know as much as that about any old feud of Shad's. Of course, Shad's got a past, and it may be lurid, but not a soul on earth knows the least thing about it, except Shadwell Dunn. How could a tame cockatoo like the professor know anything?"

"Oh, sometimes, I think that little man has a sixth sense. He sort of smells things out. And then he experiments on us. For instance, in the library this afternoon, didn't it strike you that all that description of Mr. Voorhees' hypothetical fourth-dimensional low-born murderer was more or less dragged in by the ears?"

"It didn't strike me as any sillier than the rest of the stuff he was saying. And what is more, madam, it didn't strike you either."

"It didn't impress me at the time," said my wife. "But just now—I assure you my toes were not one inch from the water in the tub—it came over me: the professor was describing a perfectly real person whose existence he had somehow come to suspect, and he was trying out the effect of the description on Shad!"

"And Shad didn't recognize the description," I said. "He was as puzzled as the deuce."

I had her there. Shad's blankness had been unfeigned, it wasn't put on. "Well, then, Shad's got a surprise ahead of him," said my wife, as she prepared to leave me. "I'm betting on Professor Ames. He knows something, Carty—that little man! He knows!"

CHAPTER XII

The next morning Ann Page breakfasted in bed and came down, a little pale, in response to a cheerful joint *billet-doux* from Freddy and Allison; they bore her off to the country club for tennis.

Shad went to keep an appointment with the sheriff, and to have an alarm sent out for a rather high-class tramp or vagrant who should not be left at large. He was swearing, with some departure from his usual calm, to run the man down. The attack on our little cousin had thoroughly roused him.

The professor looked after his disappearing car. "Mr. Dunn's state of mind is easily understandable. But I don't believe her assailant meant to harm Ann Page. Because in case he had intended to do so, there was nothing to stop him. He had taken her by surprise. She thinks she freed herself, I believe he let her go. He could have ravished and killed her—" There was a plaintive bleat from poor Gertrude, and the professor halted at once. "Oh, I'm sorry, my dear. Can't you bear for me even to say what he *didn't* do?—What is in my mind is this: Suppose the idea was only to terrify her? And through her, the rest of us? Such an attack is dreadfully upsetting to the emotional balance, the whole morale, of a household. Don't we already begin to feel that we're a beleaguered citadel? And isn't it a bad thing for the defense when the garrison begins to see red?"

"And Shadwell's seeing red this morning," said my wife. "But surely you don't mean you believe, professor dear, that the man who tried to get Shad, and got Mr. Voorhees instead, will dare to try again?" She wanted him to ridicule her own fears of last night.

He did not do so. "If once, why not twice? We'll not suggest that to Mr. Dunn, however, I think. He has plenty of agitations already."

But Shad came back considerably tranquillized. Action, even with no more immediate result than getting the sheriff started, had taken off some of his tension. Not all, though. He now had another idea. "My friends," he said, with energy, "I am about to make the Morelands come over for dinner."

"Why, Shadwell, do you think they'll want to come?" ventured Cousin Lydia, in surprise.

"I'm perfectly sure that Moreland himself won't want to, he's as cross-grained as a bear. But I shan't pay any attention to him. I'm going to make it plain to everyone in Frisbie County that we don't consider him involved in what happened here—in spite of that lunatic Hoopes. Ann Page has already arranged with Freddy to drop her at Elmington for lunch. We'll drive over for her—you and I and Gertrude together, Carter—I'll speak to Moreland then."

This programme we carried out. At Elmington, Shadwell got out alone, and went straight to the laboratory; meanwhile, Gertrude descended from her place in the front seat, and got into the rumble seat with me, in order to have my ear more accessible for low-voiced comment on the general extraordinariness of life.

We saw Shad leave the laboratory looking cheerful; he went into the house, and came out again, still cheerful, with Ann Page. They got into the front seat; Diana, slim and smiling, stood watching us from the door. "Half-past seven then!" Ann Page called back to her.—So Shadwell had got his way.

But the car did not immediately start, though we were all ready. My cousin sat staring straight before him, not touching the switch-key; Ann Page was looking at him with surprise. Then I saw a peculiar dark-red color come up on his neck, and rise all the way to his ears. And slowly, stiffly, you would have said unwillingly, as if compelled by some strong outside force, his head moved, his face turned farther and farther round toward the house, where Diana stood in the open door. He looked at her—I could see his profile now—with some unwelcome and powerful emotion that had almost the outward signs of anger; he seemed to resent whatever was obliging him to look. Then all at once he was facing ahead again, and the car leaped forward with a suddenness that nearly snapped my neck.

"My word!" breathed Gertrude, settling the hat she had almost lost. "What do you think of *that*, Mr. Carter Wing?"

Shad spoke to none of us, but drove home at top speed; he did not speak to Ann Page, he seemed not to know she was beside him.

When we reached home my wife thought that Ames should know about Shadwell's extraordinary betrayal of emotion at Elmington. "You know, professor, Shadwell absolutely has an iron will. And to see him, all at once, lose his grip on himself like that, was uncanny! The rest of us, for Shad, just had ceased to exist. We were thin air. Ann Page was sitting by him, and he never opened his mouth to her all the way home. He's tragic."

"Yes, yes, yes. Very interesting. Very interesting." Ames sounded perfunctory. "Mrs. Moreland seems to fascinate everybody but her own husband."

"Gertrude exaggerates a bit," I said. "Shad did seem abstracted, going home. But he never does talk much.—And you'll admit, my dear, that he has always been a little distant with Ann Page since she told about Isham's spying on him."

"Isham's doing *what?*" Professor Ames was not perfunctory now.

Gertrude sketched the episode, and as she proceeded, Ames sat shading his eyes with his hands, concentration in every line of him. "Go on, go on," he said nervously. "Was there anything more about Isham?" He had already heard about the fetich, and I recalled that he was an anthropologist on the side.

Gertrude was racking her brain. "Any more?"

"There was one other little trivial occurrence that he was concerned in," I said. I described the scene with the coins.

But it was to the first matter that Ames went back, and I thought he did it with an effort. He had a troubled and abstracted manner. "I've encountered a somewhat similar notion to the one that you have mentioned, my dear Gertrude, in Malaysia. Certain natives there believe that the smallest cut or scratch may be bewitched by appropriate rites, and thereafter go on horribly widening and deepening in the victim's flesh till the poor wretch dies. But I never heard it mentioned in the folklore of any African tribe."

"But what about the copper coins that were to change Shadwell's luck?" she asked him. "Is there any African folklore about that? The way the servants have fretted about the fetich is bad enough!"

He said, rather distressfully, "There must be something there. I must think—I must work that out."

Nor were our perturbations over for the day even then. About four o'clock Hoopes called up, and Shadwell being out at the time, asked for me. What he had to say was this: A poor farmer who had been driving a buggy along our road on Tuesday evening, just after nine o'clock, had seen a small truck, or possibly a station-wagon, without lights, turn out of the gate of Handsome Creek as he approached it, and dash away ahead of him, switching its headlights on as it disappeared. It had no tail-light. "Bulb unscrewed, of course," said Hoopes the omniscient. "That way, nobody could get its license number at night. Snappy work. Just tell Mr. Dunn I'm on the trail."

Shad heard the message without comment, except that he said, "Professor Ames has a right to be told. He mustn't think I allow Hoopes to hold anything out on him." And Ames made no comment at all upon his news, he only frowned and rumpled his hair. But Gertrude sighed unhappily to me when I told her, "A station-wagon!"

That evening at dinner, Moreland, extravagantly courteous to Cousin Lydia, but otherwise making no effort to hide his boredom, was the picture of a man attending a party against his will. He took half a glass of milk, and jingled his keys, and chattered brilliantly as usual, most of the time with his eyes on the ceiling; he might have been talking to himself. Diana, in her unvarying filmy black, sat in hypnotized silence, and hardly spoke at all. Nor did Shad. Unmistakably, that night, he did look broody. There was a curious inward heat glowing in the eyes that he kept for the most part fastened on the table, as he sat and crumbled his bread. Both during and after dinner, the evening was intensely uncomfortable. Shadwell hardly left Diana's side, and yet he hardly looked at her either; he sat and stared with smouldering eyes at the floor.

The professor, watching us all (I was sure) under his amiable little air of abstraction, perceptibly drooped as the evening wore on. He studied the company moodily, and admitted to Gertrude and me that his personal theory of the crime had struck a snag.

"Shall I scream in your ear again, professor?" asked my wife.

He tried to smile. "I'm afraid it wouldn't help this time, my dear. I thought I had put my finger on the thing that's the most important factor in any crime: the criminal's motive. And I've been completely wrong. The motive—or what I took for one—has vanished. Gone up in smoke. There isn't any motive at all."

The Morelands left early; I think we were all relieved to have them go. And Ames asked me somewhat peevishly, "Is your cousin Mr. Dunn quite indifferent to the amount of trouble he may make for that lady with her rather sinister-looking husband? Or is he so convinced that the hex is going to get him, that he thinks nothing matters any more?"

CHAPTER XIII

At the time of Ames' comment on my cousin's ways with Diana, we were up in our bedroom. Freddy in this troubled period had a habit of joining Gertrude and me for what he called an evening huddle. Sometimes he brought his venerable roommate (Freddy had loudly resisted all attempts to deprive him of the professor's company, declaring, "He keeps me young"). And this was one of the times.

I said, "Aren't you getting hipped on that subject of Shadwell and the hex, professor?"

"My dear fellow," said Ames, "if you think Mr. Dunn himself is indifferent to the family legend, you're wrong. I lately learned something in the village: the last surviving participator in the laying of the curse, old Sloap, the former undertaker, did not die until shortly before your cousin's return home. And I then recalled Miss Perryman's graphic and circumstantial account of Mr. Dunn's meeting with Mr. Voorhees in Johannesburg, when they renewed acquaintance over a Frisbie County paper—if you remember—"

"If we remember!" Gertrude echoed him.

"Does Cousin Lydia let us forget one detail of anything that ever happened to Shad?"

"One of those details," said Ames, "was that the paper contained an item about someone's recent death at a very great age. And it was then that Mr. Dunn announced he was going home. So I got the idea I'd like to see that paper. In the files of the *Register* office, I was able, from the approximate date, and Miss Perryman's faithful description of its contents, to identify the number that Mr. Voorhees showed your cousin. It contained, besides the paragraph about Dr. Moreland, the following lines, which I copied out."

He passed me a slip of paper. I read aloud: "Died, on Thursday, aged one hundred and two, in the Frisbie County poorhouse the county's oldest inhabitant, Waldron Sloap."

"I've been forced to change my views on some points about the unsavory Sloaps," said Ames. "But I believe that that item was what removed your cousin's objections to coming home. Objections that had persisted for years after his father's death."

"It's fantastic. It's incredible," I said crossly.

"But there really is something very odd, Carty," said Gertrude, "in Shad's exasperation and intolerance when you bring up that special superstition! Odder than just his general contempt for any kind of fear."

"It's plainly a very special case." Ames spoke in a tone of meditation. "We don't get anywhere by saying it ought not to be; that to a sensible man one superstition is like another. We don't get anywhere even by saying that black magic generally is—ought to be—a boomerang. Why, look at this very instance: these people cursed their enemy's innocent family, and death fell on their own, as if their evil will had recoiled upon themselves. But I truly believe it's useless to reason along such lines as these with your cousin. The court of last resort for any man in these matters is his own deciding mind. If he decides that he's cursed, he is cursed. He has pronounced his own sentence. His doom."

"But you meant something a whole lot less transcendental than that, professor, when you started in on this curse-thing," I said. "You meant some material and tangible threat to Shad, growing out of that old ugly affair of his father's. Your whole idea was different."

"Yes, it was different," admitted Ames. He looked worried and muddled. "But you start digging at buried lives, and you never know what you'll turn up. Like that newspaper." He rubbed his hair the wrong way, he seemed wrapped in cogitation. "Do you find, here in the South, that children brought up in proximity to the negro race acquire susceptibility to notions of that kind?"

"Sometimes," I admitted. "And the negroes were always as afraid of the whole bunch of Sloaps as if they had been the devil. They made faces going by the house in the daytime, but after dark, you bet they ran!"

"Perhaps in childhood Mr. Dunn had an ignorant negro nurse," said Ames. "There is certainly some association by which his consciousness about the hex is disturbed and discolored. It has a pathological stain. Or, to put it differently, the central idea of the curse is for some reason sur-rounded by an area of mental disturbance."

We sat there, listening to the patter of polysyllables—wondering with some affectionate amusement if the dear old boy didn't sometimes keep on talking just to hear himself talk. The operation even of Gertrude's critical mind was suspended. Ames looked so innocent, so muddled and undesigning, as he once more injected the racial peculiarities of the negro into our prob-lem, that we forgot a certain humorous warning of Allison's: "If you're ever tempted to think he's sinking into senile idiocy, that's the time to look out."

But I thought he deserved a gentle rap. "Shad's mental disturbance," I said, "isn't tranquillized by the way you forget, professor, that you mustn't talk to him about marrying and having heirs to Handsome Creek. Freddy says you did it again this afternoon!"

"Indeed he did! And this time," Freddy said, "Shad fairly growled, 'I wouldn't marry if I could, Professor Ames, and I couldn't marry if I would.' The next time, my dear professor, I think he'll simply brain you!—But why do you think he said that he *couldn't* marry? Has he got a wife somewhere?"

Gertrude said: "A man as rich as Shad can always get a divorce, silly. It's not that. Won't it be dreadful if the reason is really Diana?"

"Especially as her husband seems to be getting well!" said Freddy. "He looks better. I've noticed it."

"Yesterday," said Ames slowly, "I should have believed that there was a meaning in Mr. Dunn's words, deeper than the mere fact that perhaps he admires a married lady."

"No doubt a meaning," said Freddy chaffingly, "connected with the his-toric curse which I believe we have heard mentioned?"

But Ames didn't rise to the chaff. He said dejectedly, "I thought so. Yes. But that was yesterday."

It was the earlier part of the professor's conversation, however, that kept me awake that night. Next morning I discussed it with Allison. "And the professor isn't a negrophobe, either," I said. "He's attached to his own man Robinson."

"Attached to him? He's devoted to Robinson. Can't move an inch with-out him. And he's quite without racial prejudice of any kind."

"Something's eating him about the blacks, though," said Freddy, who was listening.

"Whatever it is," said Allison, "you can take it from me that he didn't bring it with him. He found it right here."

As it happened, Allison's last words were deeply impressed on my mind that day. All day long, I found myself watching the professor as he picked up, one by one, a succession of queer little facts that seemed to connect themselves with old Isham. It was not fancy on my part, though the vividness with which I remember them should be credited, I suppose, to an imagination uncomfortably roused and sensitized.

And I appreciate now what I missed at the time: the art with which the little wistful, puzzled-looking professor spun and wove these threads of fact together into a pattern before our uncomprehending eyes.

The process began just before luncheon when we found Shadwell, in a high state of irritability, listening to Freddy's account of Isham's queer behavior in the pantry. Shad interrupted the tale almost roughly.

"What's so funny about talking to yourself?" he demanded, in the defensive tone that he was beginning to use whenever there was an allusion to the increasingly peculiar ways of the negroes on the place.

"But it wasn't just that! He was jabbering and walking up and down *with his eyes tight shut!* Like somebody in a trance or hypnotized," said Freddy earnestly. "And there's Georgia, just as bad in her way—claims to be hearing 'voices.' Have they all gone voodoo?"

Gertrude made me a sign to look at the professor. Ames had the perfectly blank face that I had come to recognize as his sign of supreme concentration. He was waiting for Shadwell's reaction, of course. He was fairly holding his breath.

Shad said quite coolly, "If anyone is afraid of poor old Isham, I can give him a vacation." He said "afraid" in his usual tone of scorn.

"Afraid of religious hysteria?" murmured Ames soothingly. "Not in a subject of his type, I think, Mr. Dunn."

I was astonished at the unmistakable relief and almost thankfulness in the glance my cousin threw him for that suggestion. "Good Heavens!" thought I. "Is Shad as worked up about it as all that?"

"But, Shadwell," said Cousin Lydia, with gentle amusement, "I don't believe Isham would take a vacation. He'd simply refuse."

And that is what happened when Shadwell proposed it to him. Isham firmly declined to leave his place. Unless Mr. Shadwell wanted to discharge him, he added.

"You'll have to put up with him," said Shad, with some superiority, to Freddy, as the old man withdrew.

"Oh, I can do that, all right! I just want to find out what he thinks he's up to. He was at it in the dining-room too, this morning—jabber-jabber—but I couldn't get close enough—"

But at that moment the professor stumbled over the light table beside him, and sent a cascade of books and cigarettes to the floor. On purpose, I felt certain. And there was no more talk about the colored people's goings-on.

"And it was too bad of you, Freddy, to bring the subject up," said Gertrude, after lunch. "Of course the servants really are saying this house is bewitched. And what Shadwell seems to be more worried about than anything else in the world is that they may think he cares! Oh, dear, no matter how we try to go round, we stub our toes on the family curse sooner or later, don't we?" said my wife, with an accent of uneasiness that wasn't like her.

And then Ames added a little more to the puzzle. He came up to us, wearing such an odd look of excitement touched with solemnity that I asked, "Any news?"

"A sudden and most extraordinary clarification, my dear Carter. As if a door had opened in a solid wall. Exciting, but rather—terrible."

"Don't we get even a hint?" wailed Gertrude.

"The hint is that Ann Page on Tuesday evening used the telephone in the dark!"

"But, professor dear," said my wife, "if you're thinking that the murderer was in there already, and was able to keep quiet—isn't that an awful thought?—and escape detection, just because the lights weren't on then, you're forgetting that Isham went in afterwards, to look for a paper or something."

"A chap might have hid under the sofa," said Freddy.

Ames ignored the sofa. "You are right," he said to Gertrude. "Isham went in after Ann Page came out. That's so. And yet something tells me I'm on the right track."

"The track of the murderer?" I said incredulously.

"I believe so. But I still have no access to any way of proving my case to Mr. Dunn. And I fear he is merely irritated, in his present state of mind, by anything in the nature of pure speculation. I suppose it's none the less my duty to lay my conclusions before him," faltered Ames. It was plain he did not like the prospect.

"Let's say nothing to anybody until we can prove it!" exclaimed Gertrude, with sparkling eyes.

Ames said, "But until I tell Mr. Dunn himself, I feel I should not tell even you and Carter."

Gertrude was a bit dashed by that, but game. "Quite right. That's the honorable course, isn't it, Carty?"

"I suppose so," I said.

So having made us advise him to keep the whole matter to himself, as I was sure he had meant to do all along, he left us to our guesses and imaginings. "'Exciting, but rather terrible,' he said," repeated Gertrude. "I don't like the sound of that, Carter Wing. As if something monstrous were ahead!"

But a new and palpable blow that fell on us before dinner-time put out of our minds every thought of the professor's foreboding words, and even of the half-encouraging promise behind them. We learned now that Shadwell, who had separated himself from the rest of us for a short time in Washington, had done so for the purpose of seeing a doctor and had been told that his appendix ought to be removed without delay. The news made Handsome Creek look to us all in prospect like a ship without a captain. And in what a night of storm!

Shad said, however, that he was sure there was no hurry. Doctors were alarmists. He had a simple chronic condition, that was all, and had no idea of leaving till the crisis at Handsome Creek was over. "Besides, even if I did have to have the thing done, you'd have Carty in command," he pointed out, thus causing my heart to go down in my boots at the bare thought of being left in Shadwell's shoes like that.

As for Cousin Lydia, she went to pieces on the spot, and he had to promise her to make no sudden or violent motions, on pain of seeing her die of anxiety. "She's convinced the darn thing's all set to perforate if I sneeze," he said, "and she can't be reasoned with about it." He reconciled himself with a pretty good grace to the restriction, and moved about the house, as Freddy said, like a slow-motion picture of himself. There was something indescribably depressing in the unnaturalness of that slowing-down, in so vital and active a being. I know the spectacle had a measurable effect on my own nerves.

And Gertrude, too, was suffering a pendulum-swing in the direction of nameless fear. "The professor has made me wonder whether Shadwell, as a child, was ever enticed into the Sloaps' awful house, and given—some-how—a horror—!" she said unhappily.

Altogether, pessimism engulfed us that evening. There was no news of the ruffian who had terrified Ann Page, or indeed any news of any kind. Hoopes had reported no progress at all, the sheriff and his assistants were quite baffled; the murder of Voorhees, whether by mistake for Shad or by intention for himself, seemed no nearer to being avenged. The professor's hints of the afternoon now looked thin and unsubstantial under the general overhanging gloom.

And we were never for long without some small reminder of the house's tragedy. This evening it was a very small thing indeed, but it touched us with an icy finger. Gertrude, Ann Page, and I were planning to give Cousin Lydia her first lesson in contract bridge—and once again no cards were laid out on the table. There was a pause with a chill in it; I realized that no one had played cards at Handsome Creek since Tuesday night. And somehow nobody started towards the library to look for the other packs.

The professor broke the little strained hush; he said, prosaically, "Look in that blue bowl, Freddy."

Six-foot Freddy rose. The blue bowl adorned the high chimney-piece; its rim was almost level with Freddy's eyes, but not quite. "Guessed it in one!" he crowed. "Here they are!—Come clean, professor. It's a neat trick, but how did you do it? Climb on the table? That bowl's a mile above your head."

"My climbing was purely mental. And based on a simple calculation. I remembered that though you are six feet high, taller than anybody here except Mr. Dunn, somebody else in the house is taller yet. Old Isham is six foot three."

Freddy made a low bow of humility. "Frederick Gibson to the foot of the class. I should have recognized Isham's general I.Q."

"New form of religious mania?" Shadwell's voice was very odd. He turned a questioning eye on Ames. "Directed against the sinfulness of card-games?"

"And can't you picture Cousin Lydia," sang out Freddy, "doomed to spend her old age on stilts, loping from room to room in search of what-ever small articles Isham has decided are too godless to be left in her way? Come, ladies, here are the cards, have your game. Maybe tomorrow he'll burn them up!"

We chuckled at the small jest, our blood was running warmer again. We were accustomed to getting a mild amusement out of old Isham's ways. Gertrude shuffled. The professor, who didn't care to watch the game, mooned away to write letters.

But Allison presently excused himself also for half an hour, saying he had to pack some of Voorhees' belongings. And that announcement snuffed out the reviving spark of our spirits; once again all cheerfulness died. Shadwell was particularly depressed, I thought. His mind seemed far away from his surroundings. It had been so, apparently, all afternoon, for he had to apologize for completely forgetting a promise to send Freddy's car to the village garage for him; he had given both chauffeurs the evening off. He asked penitently, "Can't it wait, Freddy?"

But it was some kind of generator-and-battery trouble that had better not wait. Freddy thought he would take the car down himself, and Shad said he would follow in the Daimler, and bring him back.

Freddy protested. He could walk. By way of the quarry, it was no distance. Shad insisted; he even intimated that just now nobody ought to go about alone at night. Freddy declared that even if Shad drove down after him, he would walk anyway. "As for going alone, it's a bright moonlight night, and that path comes up across a bare field—no place for an ambush. So you can just go roll your hoop! Good grief, haven't you got any business of your own, mister?"

Shad's answer gave me a shock. "I have some business, but it won't take long; it's nothing but drafting a new will."

Nobody in the room looked at anybody else.

Was Shadwell thinking about death as seriously as that?

Freddy said gruffly, "You are not to fetch me, Shadwell Dunn. Get that?"

I offered myself in Shad's place, and was snubbed in my turn.

The end was that my cousin said, "There, spoiled child, take this, then!" and handed over a pistol from his own pocket. Another disconcertment to us all: Shad going armed!

So the matter was settled. Hard-headed Freddy was to go and return alone.

But Cousin Lydia would by no means allow Shadwell to sit in the ill-fated library alone, writing his last testament. "We'll move the card-table right in there, you shan't be by yourself."

Shad didn't get irritated, he seemed philosophical. ("Shad's too *calm*," shivered Gertrude to me. "He behaves as if he expected to die tomorrow!") He said he would collect his papers from the library, he would gargle his throat like a good boy—for he had incautiously owned to a cold, and Cousin Lydia, as usual, insisted on action—and would come back with his papers to the billiard-room. He would do these things, that is, if Freddy did not telephone that he had changed his mind.

The telephone did not ring. Evidently Freddy had meant what he said, he would be walking home.

The card-game dragged. Ann Page was watching the door. But nobody came in except Shadwell, smelling virtuously of eucalyptus, and walking drearily slow, with a lot of papers in his arm; he settled himself at a table, with his back to us, and proceeded to ignore our existence, as well as the flight of time.

I couldn't ignore the fact, however, that Freddy was staying away much longer than his business would account for. What had become of the boy?

Pretty soon Ann Page was dummy. She got up, and slipped out of the room. And I felt convicted of stupidity. Why, of course—Freddy would be waiting for her outside, he had stayed outside on purpose!—The hand went on, at Cousin Lydia's slow pace.

The hand ended. We dealt another one, and waited, and pretended that we saw nothing odd in the way the young people failed to appear. Then, just as Ames and Allison had joined us, and the professor had begun to blink and peer around and ask for Freddy, Allison, who was facing the door, jumped to his feet, with a cry of astonishment and concern. Across the drawing-room, wavering on his feet, and leaning heavily on Ann Page, Freddy came limping towards us, with a bloody face and head!

CHAPTER XIV

There was a strangled, shocked exclamation from Shadwell behind us. Freddy dropped on the sofa; he had dirt on his clothes, and indications of a badly bruised ankle in his walk, but he managed a plucky attempt at a grin.

Ann Page commanded, "Let me tell them."

She had gone as far as the terrace, she said, when, standing there in the quiet, she had heard a far-off call for help, coming from the direction of the quarry, and recognized the voice as Freddy's. And somehow, before she could think that she should have somebody with her, she was off—running like mad—down the lawn, through the shrubbery, towards the quarry.

She had found Freddy, half-conscious, on a narrow ledge just below the top of the cliff. She had scrambled down to him, and somehow, together, they had struggled back to the top. "I was glad it was dark," she said, with a shiver. "I wasn't very anxious to see that black water, eighty feet down!"

"I was ambushed all right," Freddy confessed ruefully. "The fellow must have been coming down the path, and heard me coming up, and I guess he didn't want to be seen. He scrambled up to the one possible place of concealment: the top of the bank over the path where it takes a bend; he must have been lying flat. I came up round the bend, between him and the edge of the cliff. All at once, down the bank came a section of log, rolling right at my ankles—bam!—and knocked me off my pins. In fact, he made such a good job of it that I was flat myself before I struck the edge. I rolled off along with the log, instead of toppling, and caught on that shelf. That was all that saved my life.—That, and the fact that a big stone came loose, and fell, and there was a double splash, that sounded as if Mr. Log and I had both made the trip. Lucky break. He could have pried me off of the toehold I had got in two ticks."

"But who on earth do you think it was?"

"And who did he think that Freddy was?" inquired the mild voice of Ames.

Shadwell let his breath out suddenly with a pant as if he had been running. "I get you," he said, "Same old story. You mean he took Freddy for me."

"Tosh!" said Freddy. "Look at my red hair."

"Which at night would be black," said Ames.

"That's so. And I'm tall, and my white flannels are like Shad's.—No, though! Professor, you're wrong, I was smoking!"

"Actually smoking, at the moment?" Ames was visibly taken aback.

"I had just thrown my cigarette away. But he'd have smelled it on the evening breeze! Check for you, professor."

"Always supposing he knew Mr. Dunn doesn't smoke.—Haven't you ever smoked, Mr. Dunn, at any time in your life?"

"Never," said Shad sardonically. "Don't smoke. Don't drink. Don't gamble. Model character. And yet you think somebody wants to exterminate me!" Then he rapped out, to the crestfallen professor and the rest of us, "Come, we'll take flashlights and inspect that cliff!"

We took several flashlights, we didn't reflect till afterwards that we were obliterating every footmark along the path. We inspected the bank, and the narrow shelf of rock on which Freddy thought he must have been lying for twenty minutes at least (he hadn't dared to call for help for quite a while), and we shivered; we shivered more, thinking of little Ann Page bravely clambering down, in the dark, cold with terror of the black water so far below, and cowering from the imagined clutch of some horrible hand that might any minute come out of the dark behind her!

But all that we got for our search was gooseflesh, until Shadwell pounced on a cheap cigar on the ground. It had been smoked for no more than half an inch—it seemed to have been barely lighted, and thrown away. "It's not damp. It hasn't been here long."

"So that's why our man didn't smell Freddy's cigarette," said the professor at our elbow. "He was smoking himself!"

When we got back to the house, we all went up with the professor to have a look at Freddy—including Hoopes, who had been summoned by telephone. We found my brother-in-law very comfortable in bed, with all the ladies of the house in eager attendance, and Robinson standing by with liniments.

"Catch, Robinson!" said the professor, getting rid of his automatic as usual for the night; it described a flashing arc over Freddy's bed. "And now just one question, Freddy: did you see your man at all?"

"All I saw, as I went over the edge," said Freddy, "was two arms shooting up excitedly against the sky. I saw that much by the moonlight. Not a sound—but those arms were saying, 'Good-bye—hurrah!'"

There was something quite inhuman and gruesome in that demoniac picture.

Shad's voice grated as he said, "A lot of good my pistol was!"

And Cousin Lydia, as we were dispersing to our rooms, uttered another thought that had been, I suppose, in the minds of us all. "Only think what else might have happened, too, if I hadn't made Shadwell stay with the rest of us! If somebody, prowling round outside, had looked in, and seen him sitting over his papers in the library, alone!"

Next morning Hoopes came up to Handsome Creek with an air of importance, and suggested for the second time that Shad turn his suspicions towards Allison. "You remember, Mr. Dunn, how I said he could have faked the telephone talk? And how do we know that he and young Gibson haven't quarreled over that pretty little girl, or something? If you'll note, he was out of the room the whole time that Mr. Gibson was gone. Where was he? He says he was up in Mr. Voorhees' old room, packing his stuff. But can he prove it?"

I had seldom seen Shad more exasperated. He said brutally: "Pretty soon it will be impossible for a man to go to wash his face in this house unless he takes a witness along! Good Lord, man, you've got to prove your criminal was present where the trouble was not just that he was absent from somewhere else!"

"All right," said Hoopes, "I'll do that little thing yet." He added, almost spitefully, "And the doctor was away from home last night, too. I found out."

After lunch the professor indicated that he had something to tell us that had better not be communicated to Cousin Lydia.

This time we sneaked into Ann Page's room. It was a full meeting, so to speak. Allison was on the floor, Freddy and Shad and I on the window-seat; Gertrude settled herself with Ann Page against the pillows, and the professor had the foot of the bed.

He told us he had been uncovering the weird trail of Waldron Sloap.

"I had been asking myself, in spite of everything," he confessed, "whether the body of Jefferson Sloap that was found in the quarry-pool was really a *dead* body."

Shadwell stirred impatiently.

"I beg your indulgence, Mr. Dunn. You will have your triumph presently. And you do see how that surmise fitted in, don't you? If young Jefferson Sloap had been not buried, but revived, after the accident; if he was now drawing vindictive breath on earth, a grown man, we'd have only to assume his reappearance (let us say, last week) in this neighborhood—!"

Shadwell said, in his level voice, "Inspired with the luminous idea of killing *me*."

"But as you've gathered," Ames went on meekly, "I guessed wrong. The poor drowned lad, I have learned, was very dead indeed."

Shad said, "I'm glad you're convinced. What convinced you?"

"I was perfectly certain that since the grandmother was paralyzed, old Sloap was helped by somebody in laying him out, though he was bent on having the whole credit of the job; I think he wished people to say, as some of them did, that he must have had the devil's aid. The part that he couldn't have managed alone, of course, was getting the boy into the coffin, and getting the coffin up on the trestle, all ship-shape. And I've found the negro who lent him a hand. He is scared to talk about it to this day. He ran the risk of being turned out of church, of course, if the colored people had known. Old Sloap was accused of working spells with dead men's eyeballs."

"What really happened?" I asked.

"Nothing but hocus-pocus, calculated to intimidate him. The old man told him that the 'black spirits' were present—and had a dislike of metallic objects, therefore nothing made of metal could be brought into the room; he made the terrified negro take off his Ingersoll watch and his steel-rimmed spectacles and the safety pin where his front shirt-button was off, and remove his shoes because the strings had metal tips."

"What nonsense! At least the room must have had a stove!" said practical Gertrude.

"Quite right. I told you it was hocus-pocus. But it worked. That negro's lips were sealed for years."

"How did you unseal them, professor?"

"I presented him with an infallible counter-charm against all spirits, black or white: a genuine five-dollar gold-piece"—the professor's eyes twinkled—"tied into a piece of black silk, formerly my own unworthy neck-tie. This was to be worn around the neck on a red cord for the period of one lunar month—after which the wearer must, on pain of disaster to himself, spend it immediately."

"Serpent!" gurgled Ann Page.

"By that means I learned, not only that the death and burial were no hoax, but also that the poor lad had both his eyeballs in his head, and was quite unmutilated, though battered by his fall from the cliff. 'They'd fixed him right, po' chile,' he said. 'He looked a credit to them.' And that negro was utterly honest. So there went my bright idea that the boy might have been resuscitated."

"Brrrrr!" shuddered Freddy. "If you have any more ideas as bright as that, professor, please continue to pour them into my ear only after they've been thoroughly exploded! Imagine having it suggested to you that a re-suscitated corpse, whether with or without eyeballs, was loose in the land-scape, gunning for Shadwell and tipping unidentified parties over the cliff for luck!"

"Don't!" murmured Ann Page.

Shadwell was glowering at the floor; you could not tell what his thoughts were, except that they were unpleasant. And presently he got up and said it was time for his medicine.

When he had left us, Ames said, as if he had been waiting for that chance, "So until we get a little more light on the whole subject, my dear Gertrude, you must prevail on your brother, whose red hair looks very black indeed after dark, not to go about alone at night."

"You think he's in danger?"

"I know he is."

"Then you must think Shad's in danger too!"

Ames said earnestly: "Nobody in this house is safe who crosses the criminal's trail—and anyone of us may cross it at any moment. I believe Mr. Shadwell Dunn to be already in danger of the gravest kind—and of a sort that no one present can even conceive. At this moment you'd think I needed a strait-jacket if I dared even faintly to suggest what is in my mind. And I can't speak of it in his presence, or there will be no hope of influenc-ing his actions in the manner in which—for all our sakes it may be neces-sary to try to influence them."

"You want him to go away from Handsome Creek!" said my wife.

Ames neither assented to this, nor denied it. He only said: "He has already declared that he will not go. But the circumstances aren't quite the same in your brother's case. We should really have a complication the less if Freddy would go home."

Gertrude was looking at Freddy almost hopefully. I thought she was the silliest person I had ever seen. Didn't she know anything at all about her brother? And Freddy justified my expectations. He was too much amused to be angry; in fact, he laughed out loud. "You think I'm likely to back out on Shad, the way things are, ma'am? You can think again. I'm staying at Handsome Creek till hell freezes over."

By that time it was three o'clock. Ten minutes later I met the professor coming out of the pantry door. "I've been telephoning," he said. "Where is Mr. Dunn?"

We found Shadwell. The professor began without ceremony: "My dear sir, there is something I need to do at once for my own satisfaction. It's important. Frankly, I have no notion of telling you why.—I want you and Carter to drive with me to Burnsville immediately. I'm going to talk to that young bacteriologist at the hospital."

"The one that Moreland—?" Shad's eyes widened. "But won't that be— you must excuse me for criticizing—horribly indiscreet?"

"It would be, unless I had a plausible pretext. That's why I need your help. We must have an errand, one that requires the facilities of a hospital. The simplest requirement would be for an X-ray. So we're going to say you have acute arthritis of the elbow-joint. You see?"

Shadwell saw, and from his expression he seemed inclined to think Ames had taken a liberty. But the professor's naïve and childlike air of expecting that the arrangement would suit him perfectly had its effect. When we learned that Ames had already arranged an emergency appointment by telephone, and had also asked if the bacteriologist would give him an interview, Shad yielded at all points.

"I think I'd better see my man alone," the professor explained confidingly, on the way over, "while you get your X-ray. Carty will stay with you. My interview is ostensibly to ask the young man, who has recently come back from the Orient, some questions about birdlife in Java."

And that plan was carried out. I don't suppose we were in the hospital fifteen minutes. Ames explained the excruciating (though intermittent) nature of the pains in Shadwell's left elbow, suggested the taking of several exposures, and toddled off to the bacteriological laboratory. We presently rejoined him in the hall downstairs, and were introduced to a pleasant young medico in spectacles, who seemed ready to like any friends of his new acquaintance Professor Ames.

"You'll arrange about those slides for me?" the professor asked him as we left. "So stupid and forgetful of me not to think of it till the last minute. But then I'm seventy-five, you know. Explain that it's a rush order, will you please? Price no object."

His cordial young friend said he would arrange everything.

"Delightful fellow," said the professor to Shadwell and me. "But his knowledge of tropical birds is negligible.—And I haven't the smallest intention of answering any questions of any kind, my dear Carter," he said firmly, as he saw my mouth opening to ask some. "I'm greatly obliged to both you and Mr. Dunn, and there's nothing more to be said."

And then he directed his conversation to Shadwell. "I think I should tell you, Mr. Dunn, that I have tried to make Freddy leave Handsome Creek, and that he laughs at me. He declares he won't walk out on his host. I can't convince him he is adding to your troubles."

My cousin said frankly: "He is—in a way. But I think we can take care of Freddy after this. No more trips for him anywhere alone! Besides, I'm changing my manner of dress. Don't you observe my dark-blue coat? And Freddy's forbidden to wear anything but white or very light flannels. We shan't look alike now, even at night."

I thought that the inflexible assuming of a coat of any kind, these hot evenings, was too much self-sacrifice. "For the love of Pete," I said, "now that we're all absolutely on the *qui vive*, I'd like to see the ghost of Jefferson Sloap or anybody else try to get either of you, no matter if you dress like the Gold Dust Twins."

But Shad shook his head. In the matter of the coat his mind was made up.

We were back at Handsome Creek by a quarter of six.

That evening, dressing for dinner, Gertrude sat thinking out loud to me as she brushed her hair. She sounded a little out of patience with her adored professor. "While he's talking, you not only believe that someone mistook both Freddy and Mr. Voorhees for Shadwell—you get perfectly saturated with that Greek-tragedy feeling! But even if Shad is never going to have any heirs to inherit Handsome Creek, and believes it himself, that doesn't mean he has to die! Isn't a hopeless love-affair a perfect fulfillment of the conditions—if you *have* to believe in a curse?"

"Nobody has got to. I'm beginning, though, to think that Shad himself does."

"But the professor concludes from that that Shad feels his own life to be threatened. He thinks Shad could probably tell us whom he has to be afraid of, and that the reason he won't do it is that he'd have to uncover some secret he's hiding. Well, the professor's much too subtle. Nothing is the matter with Shad personally, except that he's deeply, terribly, hopelessly, tragically in love—and it's making him so imprudent he ought to be locked up!"

And when we went downstairs, a bit early for dinner, she walked Professor Ames and me out to the safe distance of the vegetable garden for the purpose of telling him her views.

Ames said quietly, "You don't do my powers of observation justice."

"Then you agree with me?"

"I agree that Mr. Dunn is a man of strong passions infatuated with a woman that he cannot hope to marry."

"Not even if her husband dies?"

"Your cousin not only cannot at present marry the woman he loves. He cannot marry any other woman."

"Professor darling," cried my wife, "do you want me to go raving mad right here among the beans and onions? You mean he thinks he's a poor risk as a bridegroom? That he expects to have his throat cut any minute?"

"Well, I'm not satisfied that Mr. Dunn's passion alone (there's no possible doubt that he's badly in love) altogether accounts for the state he is in. It accounts for a number of things, it's an enormous complication, much more so than you guess, and makes the whole puzzle much harder to work out, because we have a whole set of factors that are open to two interpretations. His depressed looks, for instance, might be set down equally well to discouragement over his love-affair or to worry about something else."

"Yes, you can say what you like," I said to my wife, "but love or no love, Shad's mind is damn well working on something else too! I don't know whether the professor has suddenly convinced him about the curse, or whether he has had secret threats from outside that we don't know about, but he acts like a man under a doom. He feels something coming. It's as if he were sitting with his bags at the station waiting for a train that he doesn't want to take!"

We sipped our coffee on the lawn that evening; a gorgeous flamingo-colored sunset had tempted us all outside. Handsome Creek looked its loveliest in the rose-golden light.

"Isn't it a terrible thought," said Gertrude, "that maybe this wonderful house will never have a wife of Shad's in it? What with the feeling I believe he has, that he's a hunted man, and with his infatuation for a woman he can't get—"

"Sh-h!" I said, as Shad himself came out of the house, reeking of the drug-store as usual, and looking bored with life. Cousin Lydia had pounced on him because he coughed, and had sent him inside to do his duty by his throat. When old Isham took our cups from us, Shad said idly, "Didn't I hear you speaking to someone in the hall, Isham, just now?"

Isham had the air of a man who was a little puzzled himself by what he had to say. "Jus' to the doctuh, suh."

"What doctor?"

"Dr. Moreland, suh. He was goin' upstairs."

Shadwell's head jerked round towards me, with eyes of astonishment. He asked Isham, "Did the doctor say anything?"

"Nossuh."

"Did you speak to him?"

"I said, 'Good evenin', suh,' but I must 'a' said it too easy for him to hear. He just went on up. I thought somebody had been took sick—but all the family's here outside, suh."

"Had Dr. Moreland rung the bell?"

"Nossuh. Just walked in, I guess. He acted like he was mindin' his own business."

"Are you sure it was Dr. Moreland, Isham?"

"Oh, yessuh, yessuh. He walked in without no noise, like he always does—jus' smokin' his cigarette and kinder jinglin' his keys in his han'."

"When did he come down again?"

"I ain't seen him, suh. But then I've been in the pantry."

"I'll go have a look for him myself," said Shad, with careful unconcern. "Want to come along, Carty?" We went in by the portico, we went upstairs side by side. "I don't like this," my cousin said to me in a low voice. "I don't like it at all."

There was no sign of anybody in any of the upper rooms. And I didn't like the situation either. "Could it really have been Moreland?" I asked skeptically.

Shadwell stood frowning. "It's humanly possible, of course, for him to have driven up on the garden side, come in the north door, and done just what Isham said he did. But what on earth for, when he must have heard us all talking outside on the lawn?"

That was the question the others repeated when we found them assembled again downstairs: What—or whom—was Moreland's silent flitting visit for? An obscurely disquieting picture a dapper skeletal figure mounting the stairs, its footfall noiseless on the carpet. I can still feel the cold little crepitation of the spine with which I felt that impression sink in.—Stealth. No answer to a salutation. No sound but a light jingle and clink of keys.

"Gosh!" said Freddy, looking over his shoulder. Then, more vigorously, "No—that yarn sticks in my craw! I bet old Isham simply lied. Though it's impossible to see why."

"If Isham was lying," said Ames quietly, "then I never saw a man speak the truth."

"You don't suppose," sniffed Cousin Lydia, "that Dr. Moreland came deliberately prying to see if any more of Diana's jewels were upstairs?"

Allison burst out: "What do we know about Moreland, anyway? All that I know myself is that he's a rather distant cousin of Mr. Voorhees. I never saw him till we came here. Mr. Voorhees hadn't seen him for years. I don't see when or how they could have had a chance to quarrel. And yet," he said miserably, "as Hoopes said, the telephone talk does fit him. Like a glove."

Shad said shortly: "Hoopes is a nut. And, anyway, Moreland can't kill Voorhees twice over, can he?"

It was clear that he expected that to be that. I was profoundly puzzled by his behavior; he seemed to have a distrust of Moreland, and yet to be fighting it. Still wasn't that wise, perhaps! I thought of the doctor's implacable orange-colored eyes. Anybody who accused him of crime would do well to be sure he could prove the charge—or any fool could foresee trouble. Trouble that might react on Diana. I said to myself, "Shad's hands are tied."

It seemed the last straw, next morning, before breakfast, when Cousin Lydia, ice-bag in hand, and very pale, looked in from the hall to say breathlessly that Shadwell admitted he had a dull pain, low down on the right side. He vowed it wasn't much of a pain, but she was making him stay in bed.

"Oh, dear," sighed Gertrude, "I'm not superstitious, but doesn't it seem as if everything were happening at once? I've got the jumps for life. Don't drop the cap off the toothpaste tube, or I'll scream." Suddenly she lost her languor. "*Carty!* You don't think that maybe—maybe—somebody put poison in Shad's drinking-water? Or his gargle? Or something!"

I half-convinced her that poison takes a less circuitous route to the vitals than by way of the appendix. But I recognized the state of my own nerves when I found myself peering suspiciously at my coffee-cup, and wondering if the contents didn't taste funny.

Shad stayed in bed all day, and submitted to the ice-bag without a plaint. The rest of us sat about his room, played cards with him, read to him; Cousin Lydia ordered tempting trays of invalid food. By evening he said he was better. He seemed quite himself when we looked in on our way down to dinner.

Such a quiet, homely day it had been, the day that was closing. Nothing had happened at all. We lingered at the dinner-table. We were feeling a reaction and a relief after the tension of yesterday. Our spirits rose, we chatted and laughed. We decided that Isham's encounter with the doctor had been a hallucination, that Shadwell's discomfort was (inelegantly but reassuringly) gas. Hoopes, faithful, dull plodder, was on the job of avenging Voorhees—why not trust him to carry it through? He had made a silly ass of himself, from time to time, to be sure, but he would profit by the lesson. Everything was going to be all right —

Crrrash! from upstairs! *Thump!* Smaller crashes as of sliding, shattering crockery, and a climactic clang. I came up standing, I had lit three feet from my chair! And so had everybody else.—Through the hall—up the stairs—we dashed, four steps at a time and had a sharp recoil on the landing. For there in a heap at our feet, in a wreckage of china, with his head awfully doubled under him against the balustrade, lay Isham sprawled as no living man ever lay. His neck was broken.

CHAPTER XV

Cousin Lydia's maid Lena had come flying from Shadwell's bathroom, and another maid from the west bedroom corridor; and wide-eyed, barefooted, Shad had burst out of his room. No slow motion now. But nothing could be done for the poor old negro. He was gone.

I felt his heart. So did Ames. All was over. Cousin Lydia was crying on Gertrude's shoulder. Robinson, with his sad, kindly gorilla-face, helped Ames to straighten the poor head. Shadwell stood gripping the railing above us and groaned, "But, merciful Heavens!—only three steps down to the landing!" as if he saw a special malignity in a death that had happened when only a minor accident would have been predicted. The old man had been killed by a small tumble, such as very seldom kills a man. But it seemed that we couldn't count on probabilities any more at Handsome Creek.

I saw Shad's hands go up and clutch his head. "But there's no such thing as a curse!" he said, in a slow voice of horror, as if somebody had said there was. "And yet—a little short fall like that!" He looked round at me with a drawn face, his hard fingers sank suddenly into my arm. "I killed him, Carty, you know. My God, I killed him myself!"

What had happened, Shadwell explained to us when he got back his coherency, was this: Isham, leaving the bedroom on his way downstairs, with the supper-tray already in his hands, had been sent by Shad to the far end of the hall to a bookcase there; he had set down the tray on a small table that stood handy, had found the copy of *Nostromo* that Shad wanted, and taken it to the bedroom—after which he had returned for his burden. And with it in his hands, on his way past the main staircase to the service stairs, he had walked off of the top step. "If I only hadn't asked for that damn novel! Or if I had thought of it before he was right at the door with the tray! If he had left the dishes and things behind in my room while he got the book, he wouldn't have had to pass the staircase a second time. And what's more important, he wouldn't have passed it carrying something that kept him from seeing the floor in front of his feet. And yet I expressly told him, when he went back the last time, to turn the light up high! That bulb near the head of the stairs is a high-low. He turned it, too—I saw the hall get brighter. How he could have stepped right off like that, in a perfectly good light, is more than I can understand!"

Poor shivering Lena was clearing the broken dishes to one side, and Robinson, with Freddy and Allison, making ready to lift the body. Allison said: "Mr. Dunn, I was nearest the dining-room door downstairs—I got here first. And I heard a queer sound: a singular whirring noise, followed by a sort of sharp crack. That was *after* the fall, just as I was coming upstairs."

The chambermaid had heard something, too, but was too hysterical to define or describe it, except to say that the climax of the mysterious sound was not an explosion. "Mo' lak a slap." Shad had not heard it, nor had Lena. But then Lena had had a faucet running in Shad's bathroom, and the door was open between.

Ames asked, "Mr. Dunn—Paul—everybody—was the door of this armoire opposite the bookcase standing like this—half-open—when you arrived?"

The door of the ancient walnut wardrobe, ornate and carved, with an old tarnished mirror in it, wasn't really half-open, but it stood gaping enough to show the neat shelves of linen inside.

Nobody remembered about it exactly. Ames closed it thoughtfully, and the door made no sound. Rumpling his hair, he wandered over to the open bookcase where a vacancy at the end of a shelf showed that a book had been removed. The table was against the farthest wall, between the north windows; here Ames turned, apparently retracing Isham's steps. He passed to the left of the staircase, walked down to Shadwell's door and back. A straight line from door to bookshelves. He passed to the right of the staircase. A straight line from the armoire to the angle of the corridor that led to the service stairs. The hall was broad, the staircase came up in the middle; there was plenty of room on both sides. The bright light burned tranquilly over his head.

He looked past the stairhead, towards the other end of the hall. No light was burning there.

Shad caught his thought and nodded gloomily. "Yes, wasn't it a devilish combination of chances? We never keep but one burning up here, in the summer. Same old reason: the confounded gnats.—If that second light had been lighted, opposite him, right in the middle of the hall, Isham would have had something to steer by; he'd have oriented himself, and mightn't have pitched down those stairs."

We straightened the body from its ghastly position, we telephoned the authorities. Shadwell and I turned dejectedly down the hall towards his room, in slow-motion time again. His face was darker than I had ever seen it. Darker than after Freddy's narrow escape, or even Voorhees' death.

That evening there was an almost full moon. Through the end window to the south, the shade of which was up all the way, the last of the twilight looked into the hall, and already the moonlight poured its glory on the floor. It made a lovely little silver pool, and we walked through it.

"God!" groaned Shad.

Official inquiries into the disaster were quickly over. The two maids, sitting together in the little sewing-room at the end of the corridor, had been looking towards the hall. They had seen Isham cross their field of vision three times. Once carrying the tray from Shadwell's room, on his way to the bookcase. Next, going back without the tray, carrying the book. The third time with empty hands, on his way to pick up the tray again. And that time he had stopped for a moment in passing, to tell Lena that my cousin wanted her, for some small service; the remaining maid should next have seen him turning into the corridor itself, and coming towards her with his burden, on his way to the service stairs. But he had never turned that corner. Instead, there had come the crash. Death by accident. An act of God.

At midnight, after the house had quieted, but before anybody had been able to settle to sleep, I went to Shadwell's bedroom, with the other men of the household, to report that all was in order. Shad looked haggard and shaken, lying on his tumbled pillows.

The professor walked up to the bed, looking even worse than Shad, and said: "Mr. Dunn, there seemed to me to be no point in taking the authorities into our confidence at present, so I have held my tongue till now. But Isham was murdered."

Shadwell gave him a glare of stupefaction, as if unable to believe his ears. His expression said, "This little man cannot possibly be uttering the words I seem to hear." Then he sat up in bed with a spring, and said indignantly, "Of course I'm responsible, Professor Ames. I said so. But—"

"Don't excite yourself," said Ames drearily. "I'm not referring to your somewhat hysterical self-accusation, Mr. Dunn. You tell us you killed him—in a sense. Well, in another sense I also killed him. I ought to have kept this from happening. There should have been some way. For Isham did not die by accident, as the mere result of a thoughtless order. Someone deliberately put Isham to death."

Shad exclaimed, "That harmless old negro?"

"But he was all alone in the hall!" I cried.

"And he was murdered—all alone in the hall as certainly as if he had been killed with an axe."

"But nobody could have come up the service stairs," exclaimed Shad, "or even walked along the hall, without being seen by one of the two maids. And they've been there ever since their supper. Half an hour."

"You think someone came up the front stairs, Mr. Dunn? Of course you yourself and Lena and the other maid were all out of sight of that staircase," Allison said.

"But the rest of us came rushing up that way, two seconds later," objected Freddy.

Ames asked us, "Did you look about after you came up?"

Of course we hadn't looked about. No such idea had crossed our minds. Nor did Ames' suggestion seem credible, even now.

"That armoire wouldn't have held a human being," Freddy pointed out. "It's all shelves."

I said, "Professor, you ought to tell us what you're thinking!"

"It would sound fantastic, and of course there's no proof at all. No—" He looked at us with his old pinched face. "It's safer not to say."

Shad demanded, "But why in God's name should anybody have wanted to murder him?"

Ames leaned against the footboard of the bed, looking a hundred years old. "Perhaps Isham knew—without realizing that he knew—something that bore too closely upon Mr. Voorhees' death. He had to be removed before he did realize it."

We exchanged uncomfortable looks. Then Voorhees' murderer had been among us in the house—or was it merely that a confederate had been among us?

That was the night when Shadwell grimly suggested that we lock our doors.

We were gloomily separating for the night when Cousin Lydia, looking like a ruffled elderly dove in a gray kimono, descended on us with severity. Didn't we know that Shadwell was half-sick, and must get some sleep?

As she shooed us out, the hushed voice of my wife called to us. Gertrude was in bed, but she had to know what was going on. "I believe Shadwell's appendix is worse," she declared, "and you won't let me know."

She was reassured about that, however, by a second appearance of Cousin Lydia, evidently determined to hound us until she got every man into his own proper room, and the house quiet. Shad had settled down nicely, she said; she had left him falling asleep. We must follow his example. As for herself, she was feeling much relieved; Shadwell had promised to go to Washington tomorrow afternoon if he wasn't better. She had wanted him to go in the morning. "But you know how stubborn he is!—And now do send them all to bed, Gertrude!" she begged as she left us.

Then for the first time I saw Ames quite lose his self-possession. He was on his feet, his hair perfectly wild—he looked distractedly round, as if for help.

"What am I to do now? I'm too old a fellow to have to deal with this thing alone." He fairly glared at us. "Are you going to let him drop the case like this? He hasn't got appendicitis any more than I have!"

My first thought was that Ames had lost his mind. But Freddy went wrathfully straight at what the professor's speech seemed to imply. "You mean he's running away making a pretext to get out of the house? You think that of Shadwell Dunn? You can darn well think again!"

The professor was trembling all over. "And you yourself, my dear Freddy, haven't even begun to think!—Running away? Mr. Dunn is past fear, he is even past caution. He is lying to all of us, he is making a pretext, yes—but a pretext to commit an enormous imprudence. He is rushing upon a deadly risk that till now he has steered clear of. I know it! I'm sure of it!"

"What risk? What imprudence?" I demanded. "When you tell us that Shadwell's lying, you've got to explain."

"Do I need to explain that your cousin is a man in the grip of a passion? And faced with an obstacle? He is going to tackle that obstacle, at no matter what cost—he can't wait. And how are we going to stop it?"

Gertrude cried, "I can't believe Shad's lying! He looks ill, he looks wretched."

But over Freddy's dazed face a look of understanding broke, though it was an unwilling and revolted understanding. "Then you mean the obstacle is simply—Moreland? And Shad cold-bloodedly wants to be out of the way when his man Hoopes hands him over to the sheriff? David-and-Uriah business? Oh, come!"

Ames had stopped trembling now. His pale old features were like stone. He said to me: "I'm about to write a note to your cousin, which I intend to put under his door as I go by. You shall all read it. May I use your desk?"

The completed note, which I read aloud, was as follows:

> Dear Mr. Dunn:—I have the honor to request that you and
> Mr. Hoopes, who of course is under your orders, will meet
> me tomorrow morning at twelve in Dr. Moreland's labora-
> tory. If for any reason it is disagreeable to you to join us, I
> will see that Mr. Hoopes has time to report to you on the
> morning's proceedings before you take your train.
>   Very truly yours
>   Leonidas Ames

Gertrude said, "How you do know Shadwell! He'll come if it kills him."

CHAPTER XVI

Next morning Shadwell did not appear, and we learned he had been closeted in his room with Hoopes since seven o'clock. Ames received word before breakfast that both of them would meet us at Elmington.

We had two other bits of news as well, both of them somewhat upsetting. The first one was that my own admirable Gertrude had "leaked" to Cousin Lydia. Moved by the dear old lady's dismay on hearing that Shadwell planned to get up and dress hours before train-time, my wife had told her the reason; and Cousin Lydia, with her accustomed force of mind, at once ordered a car to be ready to take her to Elmington at twelve.

There was nothing for the professor to do but to send word to everybody else concerned that the time was changed to eleven. Everybody, that is, except Freddy. That young man had what his sister hoped was a very special date for a stroll with Ann Page at eleven. Very well, Freddy could come along, as scheduled, later. Surely our posse was large enough for anything! And as a matter of fact perhaps no posse, however large, could have prevented what happened in Moreland's laboratory before we left it.

The second bit of news came in the form of a memorandum submitted by Hoopes to Shadwell, and sent on to me by my cousin without comment; he was getting me ready to assume command at Handsome Creek after he took the train. A horribly depressing prospect. The memorandum said a small garage on the edge of the village reported that on Wednesday morning Mrs. Moreland's gardener had stopped there, and bought a headlight bulb for her station-wagon.

"I fear," said Ames, "that the time has come when we must begin to take Mr. Hoopes' activities more seriously. Will you and Gertrude come for a stroll with me after breakfast?"

He conducted us first to the left of the big gate, where it was by this time becoming all too evident that Diana must have parked her station-wagon on Tuesday night. As Hoopes had said before, there was no sign that any car had stood there. "But Georgia and Miss Lydia between them have established the fact pretty well, I'm afraid," said Ames. He led us then a little nearer to the house, where a group of young spruce made a cover, and there on the grass was a dark patch of heavy grease, unmistakably from a car. "Recent, but not fresh, you see. It has been rained on, but it will take some time to wash away; the quantity is large for a mere dripping. Presumably the car also was large, and in bad repair, or it would not have lost so much oil in a short time. Now suppose we check up on something else."

I could guess where we were going now: to the place where Gertrude had seen Moreland's cadaverous head watching his wife across the hedge. And sure enough, there on the grass again was another big patch of oil.

I rather wondered at the loud tone of satisfaction in which Ames went on: "I had noticed a very large stained area in front of the door at Elmington. I should say the doctor's car drips badly, right along."

A gratified male voice from the other side of the hedge said: "Thank you for the tip, professor! I wondered what you were looking at with Mr. and Mrs. Wing. Now I think I can ask for the arrest of Dr. Moreland."

We heard the heavy, crunching footsteps of Hoopes on the gravel drive, as he strode away.

My wife's shocked face—and my own, I don't doubt, as well—made a strong contrast with Ames' little quiet smile. He said, in his natural voice: "Of course he was morally certain to eavesdrop, after he'd spied us from the windows. We'll give him a lesson.—And now we must find Ann Page."

Ann Page was mistrustful and defiant, upon first approach. When Ames said to her, "My dear, we need to know everything you know about Mrs. Moreland, especially her correspondence, and we need to know it at once," she retorted, "Ask Diana for yourself!"

But Gertrude told her what Hoopes had said to us through the hedge, and she turned rather white.

"All right," she said shortly, angry tears rising in her eyes. "You don't know what you're doing—hounding her like this. Yes, I've taken letters to the mail for her. And letters have come for her, addressed under cover to me. Is that what you want to know? They were quite all right. She was writing—"

"Part of the time writing to Burnsville, about something her husband thinks she doesn't know?"

Ann Page was too agitated even to be surprised. "Yes! And part of the time to his own uncle—the one that he hates so. There!"

Moreland's mother's brother was a notorious crooked politician in Pennsylvania, vastly disreputable, vastly bland and easy-going, vastly rich. Moreland, it seemed, had denounced and disowned him. That was the sort of uncompromising, cantankerous thing that Moreland could be counted on to do. But the old man, who liked Diana, was paying the Burnsville doctor to save his life.

"She can't let him know! And there's more to it than that. Every penny of Dr. Moreland's money is gone, since the big crash. They are paupers, but she makes-believe, somehow—I don't know how she contrives it, I suppose she has a tiny tiny little bit of something of her own. Colonel Milton, the dreadful old man, has offered him an allowance, but he refuses. You can't imagine the straits they're in, and he lives buried in his laboratory, writing—she doesn't let him know. Dr. Ames, she pays her servant, her mulatto girl, by making her clothes for her! Yes, that proud lady! She pays for gasoline by teaching music to the garage-man's little girl. She pays her gardener with three fourths of the garden-stuff—he peddles it. Oh, she's giving her husband every chance for his life, but when he recovers, I hope she shakes the dust of his hateful house from her feet—"

"But her own marvelous clothes! That yellow dress! Those things cost a fortune!" cried Gertrude.

"She knits them herself, every stitch, sitting up night after night. And have you ever seen her wearing anything else? She washes them herself, when you and I and Dr. Moreland are fast asleep in bed! She has one black evening dress, just one, that soft, fluttery thing that makes her look like a queen.—But she'd look like a queen if she were dressed in old newspapers!"

Ames prevailed on Ann Page to arrange for him to talk with Diana. "I shouldn't be seen talking to her," he said, "and time is terribly short. Can you ask her to meet Carty and me in the wood by the quarry?"

Diana came stepping proudly through the wood where we were waiting for her. She was deathly pale. As if tired of pretense, she was this morning shabby though immaculate in a very old and mended white dress. She sat upon a large stone, and Ames and I upon a fallen tree.

"Mrs. Moreland," said Ames, "I am here to tell you certain things I know, or have surmised, and you will then—as you value your husband's life—fill in the rest."

She looked at him in silence, breathing quickly. How much, after all, did she value Moreland's life?

"You asked Mr. Voorhees to sell a jewel for you, without the knowledge of your husband. It was all you had left. And your husband saw you in conversation with him."

Horrified astonishment flared up in her eyes. This was a misfortune she had not guessed. Perhaps she remembered her tears.

Ames went on: "That afternoon Mr. Voorhees found that he must leave Handsome Creek immediately. He hurried to your house, and left something with the maid for you: an ordinary road-map. But folded inside it without explanation, because he had no time to write—I believe there was an advance on the price of your diamond frame. A hundred-dollar bill. And Dr. Moreland found it. He brought it back to this house that night at about fifteen minutes past nine."

There was no increase in the horror of her look, for that would not have been possible, but something in her ravaged face said, "I begin to understand!"

"You received the innocent-seeming map. At the same time you became conscious of a deep displeasure—deeper than ever before—in your husband, and you were mystified. During the card-game that evening, you learned that Voorhees was out for dinner, and being frantic with anxiety to see him, you got rid of your guests and drove off to Handsome Creek, leaving the lights in the house so arranged that when your friends came back with the medicine they would think you had gone up to bed. When you got here, you parked near the gate, hoping to see Mr. Voorhees come in that way. But he must have come up by the path. You missed him. Presently, however, you saw your own husband's car come in at the gate, without lights, drive closer to the house than your own position, and stop. And following your husband up to the house, across the terrace—looking in the library window—you saw him with Mr. Voorhees. I mean you saw him with the dead body of Mr. Voorhees. Am I right?"

She inclined her head.

"So we know—you and Mr. Wing and I—that matters may become awkward for your husband, if he is arrested for the crime. There is no evidence that Dr. Moreland wielded that knife, but neither is there any evidence that he did not. And the hundred-dollar bill is against him."

"My husband is not a murderer," said Diana steadily. "He is possibly capable in his heart of killing an enemy in a fair fight—I don't know—sometimes I think I know less of him than I do of anyone in the world. He has become a mystery to me. But I know he would not stab his bitterest enemy in the back."

"Your saying so is to his credit," said Ames. "It is even more to yours. I am your very admiring humble servant, Mrs. Moreland."

Deep color rushed over her bloodless face, and her eyes brimmed. This woman could be stoical under cruelty, but kindness made her a child. She stood up, trembling. "What do you want me to do?"

"Only to trust me, and believe me when I tell you that your fight to give your husband a fair chance is over. Your duty is done. He is recovering."

Impossible to know what this meant to her. The mask was on her face again. With a deep breath, "I will trust you. But I am—very tired. Try to let the end come quickly now," she said; and left us.

"I noticed that you didn't tell her about Moreland's other appearance at Handsome Creek," I said. "When Isham saw him go upstairs. What about that? One secret visit might be innocent enough. But there were two!"

Ames rumpled his hair. "I must ask you also to trust me," he said.

When Ames and Allison and I entered Moreland's laboratory at eleven the next morning, we found him waiting for us. And we were surprised when Diana entered just behind us. Close after her, also with looks of some surprise, came Shadwell and Hoopes.

Moreland said formally: "I asked my wife to join us when Dr. Ames and his party came. It is important that she should have no illusions about the position I am in. You are here, I suppose, professor, to notify me that the sheriff is coming to arrest me for murder."

"The sheriff is certainly coming, Dr. Moreland," said Ames, without embarrassment. "And with your permission I shall presently introduce another person, unknown to all of you. To all of you, that is to say, except Mr. Dunn."

My breath came faster. This was exciting, this was the end! The mystery of Shadwell's ambiguous reticence would soon be a mystery no more. I thought my cousin's composure strange. If he was perturbed, I had never seen a person conceal it better. Ames' speech made no apparent impression on him at all. His overnight decision, since the dire shock of Isham's

death, to take whatever perilous step the professor thought he was planning, seemed to have uplifted and steadied him.

He merely said: "I hope the person is interesting. I've known some very
dull ones. More stuff about the well-known hex, I suppose?" with the in-
difference of one immersed in other thoughts that were both more absorb-
ing and more pleasant. "Whatever Shadwell's project is, in Washington,"
I thought, "he thinks it's what the case requires. He believes in it." Then I
had a queer twinge. Did my cousin's satisfied and tranquil air mean that
Moreland was going to be locked up? I didn't—I still couldn't—believe that
would happen.

But Moreland believed it. He turned to Diana. "I am to be arrested for
the murder of Matthew Voorhees," he said. "I shall probably be hanged.
Think of me as a dead man, and speak the truth, as God made you: how
much money have you had from my Uncle Stephen?" A check-book appeared in his hand.

"Richard! Not here! Not now!"

He appeared not to hear her. "As family treasurer, you have kept me
informed on the state of my diminished income."

("Diminished?" I said, aside to Shadwell. "Ann Page distinctly said
there was nothing left."—"Diana lied to him, then," Shad said. "Women do.")

Moreland went on. "You are a clever manager. We have had a roof, and
food, and service. But how much have you been accepting from my uncle,
Colonel Milton, to buy your beautiful clothes?"

She began to tremble. "A—a reasonable allowance."

"*How much?*"

She named a sum. Her low voice had the accent of utter truth. "You
do him credit," he said smoothly. "I thought it was more." He scrawled a
check. "I'm a dead man now, Diana. Swear to me that you'll send him this
at once."

"But we haven't this much in the world, Richard—"

"What's that? Why haven't we?" She bit her lip. "I suppose you mean,"
he said, "that we've none to spare for such a purpose. But this check isn't
made out against our joint account, I'm not robbing you. It's drawn against
a new account of my own, just opened, earnings of a silly book of 'Travels
in the Orient'—gossipy trash for globe-trotters—that I scribbled and hardly reread. God, it's swill! But making money, my dear! There'll even be
something for you as a widow." To Ames he said: "Excuse the business

conference. I wished my wife to realize that the end was here at last—in your person. Now I'm ready."

She would have protested, I thought—entreated—uttered some plea, but the weight of his unearthly coldness bore her down. He despised her, but she dared not come out with the truth. If she told him she had been penniless, and had tried to sell the diamonds through Voorhees, she would be also telling Hoopes that Moreland had found and misunderstood and resented the hundred-dollar bill. She would be putting the rope around his neck. She fell back.

He repeated, "I'm ready. Where's the sheriff?"

"My dear doctor," said the professor agreeably, "there seems to be some slight mistake. We are not expecting the sheriff for quite a while. Nor have I said that he was coming for you."

"You are not charging me with the murder of Voorhees?" Moreland demanded.

"Not at present."

"And yet," he said recklessly, "I suppose you know that I was in the library at Handsome Creek on Tuesday evening at a quarter past nine?"

"The exact time of your visit was not known to me, doctor. But I presume that—ah—that you found life was extinct?"

Moreland nodded, looking more and more bewildered.

"I thought so," said Ames. "I suppose you did not manipulate the radio?"

The doctor shook his head.

"But *somebody* manipulated the radio after fifteen minutes past nine!" I exclaimed. "And if Voorhees was dead already—"

Ames interrupted me blandly, to ask Diana, "May we sit down, Mrs. Moreland? And I hope you won't leave us yet. Your presence may be helpful.—Doctor Moreland, we need a little counsel about the psychological side of the outrages that have been occurring at Handsome Creek."

It seemed to me that my brain must be turning. I had expected to see Moreland confronted with proofs of his crime, and here we were, asking his professional advice! He seemed as much at sea as I was, and said stiffly, "I am not a psychiatrist, Dr. Ames!"

"Nonsense, nonsense!" said Ames, with a vaguely optimistic gesture. "You're enough of a psychologist to answer a question: am I right in thinking I see in our criminal clear evidences of a disintegrating mind?"

"You mean he's a maniac?" inquired Shadwell. "Just killing at random? Good! Then you've given up the fantastic idea that he's after me!"

"Suppose we look at these diversified outrages," said Ames. "Four of them in a row. The first one has the appearance of a business-like murder done for a reason. Its distinctive characteristic is—shall I say—its neatness. No brutality, no lost motion.—Do you follow me?"

We all did. Of course he was right.

"The other acts of violence that have occurred are different. Not only different from the murder of Mr. Voorhees, but different from one another. The terrorizing of Ann Page was quite uncalculated and impulsive, since the assailant could not have known she was coming out of the house; it was (I am convinced) not murderous at all. But by the time that we reach the attack on Freddy, our man is savage. All worked up—perhaps against everyone belonging to your household at Handsome Creek, perhaps even (how do we know?) against the whole human race. I say this, because it's unlikely that anyone has a sensible, sane grievance both against Freddy and against you. The remaining possibility—unless we have two separate criminals to deal with, which seems preposterous—is that he mistook Freddy for yourself. As he may have mistaken Voorhees for yourself. But that still doesn't explain the difference in what I may call the atmosphere of these two occasions. The murderer who killed Voorhees was cool and self-possessed, but when Freddy was attacked, the attacker was excited. All this points to a steadily diminishing power of self-control."

Shad thought this over in silence. Then he asked, "What about Isham?"

"Ah, that's more complicated! I'm convinced that Isham's death was in the true sense not exactly a murder. He was intentionally precipitated down those stairs, in cold blood, by someone who meant him to be serious-ly injured—in fact, to be incapacitated for a time—but I do not believe his fall was intended to cause his death."

Shadwell drew a great gusty breath that had a sound of relief, and I felt a lifting of my own heavy spirit too.

"That takes away some of the beastliness," I said.

"Still, you see my point," said Ames. "Our man strikes more and more wildly. Takes more and more chances. There is bound to be a reason."

Shadwell had all along been narrowly watching the doctor. The knowl-edge of Moreland's presence in the library had come to him as a complete surprise, and I wondered if he was remembering Moreland's later secret entry at Handsome Creek which had not been explained.—As for Ames' behavior, that I had given up trying to understand.

He now turned unexpectedly to what seemed to me to be a brand-new subject. "And to clear up your troubles at Handsome Creek, Mr. Dunn, I warn you that you must first bring the morale of your household back to normal. It's important to get the negroes pacified."

Shad bristled instantly. I don't see the importance."

"You'll get no intelligent co-operation, my dear sir, until you do. You'll not even get truthful reports on what actually happens in your house or on your land. Perhaps the reports will be meant for truth, but your people are no longer able to see or hear straight. It's almost an hypnosis. Anybody who plays on their persisting terror of that old man, though he's in his grave, can make them believe anything."

"What old man?" said Shadwell forbiddingly.

"Why, the old conjuring undertaker, of course. The one with second-sight."

"Second-sight!" sneered Shad.

"But he did have it, my dear sir. There are certain things that cannot be explained away."

"Sloap's tale isn't one of them, though! That's one thing I never intended to tell, but I may as well put an end to this lunacy now. Old Sloap didn't need second-sight to tell him I'd run away from school. He had seen me!"

I thought the professor had the oddest expression I had ever seen, so many emotions mingled in it. The ruefulness alone was plain. "I really thought," he said softly, as if to himself, "that I was at the bottom of the surprises. And now this comes.—May I ask—"

"I had run for home, I tell you! Afraid of home, but more afraid (or I thought so) of the rest of the world. But when I got in sight of Handsome Creek, where I knew my father's leather belt was hanging ready for me in his dressing-room, I funked it. I saw a light in the Sloaps' filthy kitchen, and I knocked. I had been inside there before.

"Old Sloap let me in. Jeff wasn't at home, he said. No one knew yet where Jeff was—that night. But he was not a hundred yards away from us right then, while we talked. With his head under water." Shad's voice had a strong shudder in it. "Sloap gave me a soggy piece of apple pie to eat. Stale. I can taste it now. It seems to taste of the quarry-pool.

"He scared me out of going home. Of course I realize today that he did it on purpose. He talked about that leather strap, and—other things. He had a vile imagination. My father wouldn't have done those other things, but I was a coward then, you know." The "then" had an angrily defensive ring. "I let Sloap terrify me. The ship was his suggestion, and the postcard to Jeff; he wanted the fun of taking it up to Handsome Creek. And he carried that part of it out, after Jeff was dead. Well, that's all! But what price second-sight now?"

"The second-sight," said the professor meekly, "seems to be out."

"I stood there in that dirty kitchen," said Shad, "and thought about the pleasant rooms at Handsome Creek, up the hill. The soft, clean beds. I longed for them as if they had been something in a dream, that I had wanted and never had." Shad's voice had a savage bitterness. "I knew that maybe as long as I lived I'd never lie in a room, or in a bed, like those up there. And I tucked my tail between my legs, and turned my back on them. Are you surprised that I swore to myself I'd never tell?"

I had lost the capacity to be surprised at anything. So Ames had been right when he connected Shad's long delay with Sloap, though he had got the reason wrong. Shad had shrunk from the sight of the ancient wretch, and from his hateful glee over how his enemy's son had run away a second time from his father's very door! Could any man have borne those jeers? Never! Shad had waited till Sloap died.

"That explains a puzzling point," said the professor, rallying. "There you were, looking back across the sea at Handsome Creek, wishing you could come home; but Sloap stood in the way. So you had to wait."

Shadwell colored angrily. This was a slur on his pluck, not in the remote past, but in a past that was recent. The professor, however, gave him no time to speak. In a tone of cheerful unconsciousness he said: "We will not repeat your story, I think, outside of this room. As a fresh instance of the old rascal's force, it might unsettle your people still further. Already they believe that you are expecting the worst."

"The worst?"

"From the hex, of course. They are convinced of it. They say you wear a charm against it day and night, it never leaves you—a bracelet of copper wire on your left arm above the elbow, with a copper coin bound onto it in a special way."

Shad snapped, "What special way?"

"I'm only telling you what they say," said Ames gently. "Robinson is my authority. They think you wear that coat now to conceal the charm."

"I wear this coat," said Shad, "so as not to be mistaken for Freddy, or have him mistaken for me. And you know it."

"Of course, of course," said the professor rather flutteringly. "But to their ignorant minds it's a sign of panic. A sign that you're afraid of the hex at last."

A spasm of real rage passed over Shad's face, and I felt that Robinson, the too-faithful reporter of these things, was lucky not to be there. But the professor went on: "According to Robinson, they describe the charm in some detail. The copper coin is a penny, pierced with seven holes in a pattern which no one will draw for him, but which of course has a meaning, probably obscene. Through the holes it is bound to the wire—with seven black horsehairs. I learn," the professor said, with childish delight, "that a horsehair thread is the only one that bad spirits can't bite through! Wonderful bit of folklore that!"

"Damn it all!" exploded Shadwell, "Come and *feel* my arm!"

He meant it too. Allison and I obliged him. Naturally there was no bracelet or coin of any kind. Shad was beginning to recover his equanimity; he even laughed, though sourly. "Don't you want me to undress for you?" he asked. "Maybe I'm tattooed somewhere in a design"—he shot a wrathful look at Ames—"that's probably obscene!"

The professor managed to combine deprecation with firmness in his vague old voice. "But in spite of your sarcasm, my dear sir, we still need to humor the ignorant. I think I have the means of doing so, right here in my pocket. And of showing that you don't wear charms. The Burnsville Hospital has made me a slide of the X-ray picture of your arm; of course it shows you are wearing nothing of the kind.—Will you put it in your projector, Dr. Moreland?" He held out an oblong plate of glass. "We'll take a look at it."

Moreland, surprised but courteous, accepted it. He wheeled out the projector, and switched the current on. He turned the slide in his fingers, getting it right side up.

Suddenly a loud, startled oath burst from Shadwell, and I saw his forehead knot into ridges of fury. He took a stride

Ames' voice crackled, "Put it behind you, Moreland!" Not a second too soon! As Moreland automatically whisked the plate out of sight, a pistol barked, filling the room with acrid smoke. And back of where Moreland's hand had been, a black hole in the wall showed where the bullet went in.

We were all, for a moment, paralyzed. Frozen. Shad, over his still-leveled automatic, and Moreland, with the slide held behind him, glared at each other, two figures of fury. And of us all, Diana sprang first. She was on her husband's breast; her arms clasped round him held his arms down to his sides. She was sobbing, "Not without me!"

"Get away, Diana!" he cried in agony. "Take her away, somebody. That lunatic will kill us both."

"They can't take me! I will not let them.—Shadwell Dunn, fire again now. I'd rather die with Richard than live another minute like these last months I've lived."

"He won't fire, Moreland," said the astonishingly calm voice of the professor.

All of us but Diana were looking at Shadwell. His eyes never left Moreland's eyes, his automatic was trained on Moreland. But the professor repeated: "He won't fire. Not while you don't move. It isn't you he's after."

"Richard," sobbed Diana, "if Shadwell Dunn has gone mad, and kills us both, I don't care. I've never had a happy moment since you ceased to love me.—I disobeyed you, and wrote to your Uncle Stephen. I had to! We couldn't have lived. All your money was gone, every penny of it. Swept away. I lied when I told you I was letting him give me a dress-allowance. I took his money, but it was to buy our bread—to let you have your chance to live! Oh, I've died a thousand deaths, lying to you—pretending I was squandering it on my indulgences, my clothes! I don't care whom you've killed, or what you've done. If you killed Matthew Voorhees, it was a good deed. If you ever killed any man, he deserved to die. You are the only living soul I've ever known who didn't know how to do wrong!—But now that they've learned you were at Handsome Creek that night, ask Shadwell Dunn to fire, and have it over."

"Diana—dear!" His voice broke. "Please, you fellows, take her away."

"Mr. Dunn," said the professor, "it is very much to be regretted if Dr. Moreland did kill Mr. Voorhees, but Mrs. Moreland is out of it. Will you put that pistol down?"

Shadwell might have been deaf; all of him was concentrated in his eyes. And Diana might have been deaf, with her head on Moreland's breast.

"Darling," she said, "if Shad wants to kill you, he must kill me too—and I want you to know I love you—I'd wear rags for you—"

One of Moreland's arms came free, and clasped her, and then, as her arms moved upward and met tight round his neck, his other hand and arm, that had been behind him, rose to complete the embrace.

Too late the professor snapped, "Down with that plate, Moreland!" Shad's automatic had cracked just a split second more quickly; the plate of glass flew into splinters, and down the side of Diana's white dress a thin red stream of blood trickled from Moreland's right hand, deeply cut by the fragments, as he crushed her to him. Their dazed eyes, when in the silence they looked round, and found they were alive, showed how far they had been from that room.

Shad, breathing fast, said, with a sort of harsh punctiliousness, "Sorry I cut your hand, Moreland, but I'll not be made a show of."

"And since the slide's gone," said Ames resignedly, "and Mrs. Moreland seems so alarmed, may we have an end of the gun-play, Mr. Dunn? May I have that pistol?" He held out his hand.

Shad gave a short laugh. "No," he said, "but here it goes!" The next minute it had spun gleaming out of the open door, and a silver splash showed where it struck the river.

"That's better," said Ames. He was standing in the door now, facing us, his hand was in his pocket. "Moreland, you got a look at that slide, of course. What was on it?"

"Why, nothing," said Moreland, astounded. "I mean, nothing out of the way."

"Ordinary everyday muscle and bone, and so on? No bracelets or copper coins? Nothing to remark upon? Just exactly like a million other people's arms?"

"Certainly."

Shadwell's already angry face had been growing darker as he listened. He said abruptly and violently, "Let me pass, you little madman!" He advanced towards Ames.

The professor gave a sharp whistle. Silently out of the mass of lilac bushes beside the door rose the form of Robinson. The colored man's long-armed, sturdy figure stepped past the little frail one that made room for him.

"Robinson, you know what we have to do."

"Yessuh."

"And after you have done whatever job Professor Ames has for you to do here, Robinson," said my cousin threateningly, "you and I will have a talk about this interesting story of the charm and the horsehairs and the arrangement of holes that is probably obscene."

"About what, suh?" Robinson's eyes turned for orders towards the professor.

"Robinson won't be able to help you, Mr. Dunn. As a matter of fact, I was surprised that you believed a word of that stuff. It wasn't very clever—even though I made it up myself."

"Made it up—yourself?"

"Every word."

Shadwell's rage was rising higher. "And with what object may I ask?"

"Frankly, I had hoped that your exasperation would be acute enough to keep your mind occupied, and prevent your realizing what was on that slide—or rather, what was not on it—until we got it on the screen. Then we should not have needed to—"

An imperceptible movement of the professor's hand was Robinson's cue. The next instant, the room was a pandemonium of grunts and tramplings, over which rose the unmistakable sound of some tough stuff being rent and torn. The three struggling bodies flung apart as suddenly as they had flung together; the professor, still staggering, with half of a dark blue coat in his hands, was upheld by Robinson's arm. And Shadwell, who had wrenched his wrists free from the negro's viselike grip, had not done it in time to stay the professor's knife at the back of his collar, or the professor's two wiry hands that had split coat and shirt from his back, and dragged them forward from his shoulders. His magnificent torso was bared—the grand muscles still tense with struggle, the ribs heaving under the cream-white, unflawed skin of the sides—where there should have been a red-and-purple furrow

"Steady!" panted the professor, above his own leveled automatic. "Steady, there—Jefferson Sloap!"

CHAPTER XVII

The splendid half-naked figure that faced him gave a sound between a wild laugh and a curse. "Now that you've got me, I wish I had time to hear how in hell you did it."

"Time?" breathed Diana, shrinking, and slipped her hand into Moreland's, as if in terror of still more violence to come, more threats against her beloved. And Robinson moved towards the door, to take upon himself the shock of any assault upon that way of escape. The professor, however, seemed to take his captive's words in a different sense, and with a grave and courtly nod accepted that meaning. The bare-breasted giant, who had suddenly ceased to be Shadwell Dunn, far from making a rush at the door, actually backed away from us as far as the opposite wall; there, with folded arms, he leaned back against the shelves of chemical supplies. He said coolly, "I suppose the sheriff really is coming?"

Ames said, "In twenty minutes."

"Okeh. Tell me as much about it as you can. Talk fast. I mean it. I thought I hadn't left a trace."

"You hadn't. Not a material trace, that is."

The other man gave a sort of strange sigh of gratification. "Glad of that, anyway. But you made a monkey of me over that X-ray! No sign of any former break in the bones—was that it? Damn clever. But whatever got you to the point of suspecting?" Suddenly the speaker halted. "Mrs. Moreland," he said, with formality, "your husband is in no danger from me. Will you do me a last favor? Go quickly back to the house, and meet my—my aunt Lydia when she comes. You'll greatly oblige me. Don't let her come any farther. She has been mighty good to me." As Diana loosed the hand she was holding and slipped out, he turned back to Ames, "When did you guess?"

"I suspected you immediately. But I'd like to be told how the original substitution came about."

My illegitimate cousin—how strange to think that the relationship was unchanged, except in the abstract eye of law!—said: "It was really an accident. He—the other one—came home, when he ran away from school, and didn't dare go in. I found him up on the quarry-path, that night, pretty near dawn it was, sitting on a stone, trying to get up his nerve. I was half-drunk, and eating a piece of apple pie I had stolen, and he ordered me to give it to him. We fought and I threw him and cracked his skull on a stone. And then, being drunk, and as tall as he was, though I was so much younger, I got the idea of dressing up like him—I dreamed I could carry it off! Well, my old uncle came wabbling along and pricked that bubble. Of course, my only hope was to run. He instructed me to write the postcard, and he did the rest. A rare time he must have had! I can fairly see him smack his lips to think how much worse he was punishing Avery Dunn than by letting him know his son was dead!"

"Your own very striking abilities seem to be inherited," said Ames dryly. "That trick of your uncle's for getting the negro's spectacles off, to prevent his recognizing the other boy when they laid him out, was masterly. And of course it was on account of the old man that you wouldn't come back."

"I'd have been right under his thumb, wouldn't I? It was tantalizing, though, when I began to be sure I had grown up more of a Dunn than—the other one." Through the whole of this strange interview, the false Shadwell never called the true Shadwell by his name. "I knew that. I knew it long before Voorhees thought he recognized me in South Africa, when he had never seen me in his life, any more than I had him. And now, *your* tale! Quick!"

Impossible to describe the mingled fascination and horror of seeing the person you had known change, feature by feature as it were, into another man! And now we were to hear how Ames, that first midnight, had gathered the truth from Gertrude's story.

"The first clear indication that pointed to you," said Ames, "was the radio programme."

"I don't follow."

"I found that Carty had been sitting on top of the evening paper from before the return of Mr. Voorhees till after the murder was discovered. In other words, when the music started, the paper was not available for reference. Yet you, a music-hater, not given to the study of radio pro-grammes, instantly knew not only the selection but the singer's name. Ergo, for some reason you had become familiar with that number in advance."

"Hardly conclusive."

"Something a little more conclusive was to see the Assistant Secretary of Agriculture talking on another station at the same hour! You had lied about the time of that talk on hogs. Why?

"I didn't get the answer to that for two days. But in the meantime what clinched my suspicions was the telephone talk. Perhaps you are familiar with that saying of a well-known scientist: 'Never admit a complex expla-nation till all the simple ones have been tested and found inadequate.' I performed a simple qualitative analysis of Mr. Voorhees' end of that di-alogue: I sifted out the actual, literally quoted words of the speaker, and separated them from the interpretations that the various commentators—beginning with you, my dear Paul—put upon them. Let us see what they are: 'All wet . . . transparent . . . sticking to you . . .' Now the moment one gives up trying to be clever about those words, and allows them to say what they mean, one has a picture of literal wetness and adherence and trans-parency, and 'sticking to you' unmistakably indicates a garment."

I was getting a feeling, almost of delirium, which cleared up, however, with the professor's next words: "But Voorhees wanted to be sure; he tried to tear the shirt down the back."

I fairly heard the jerk as Hoopes' jaw dropped. Even his monumental complacency took a jolt from that. "His wet shirt sticking to his ribs!—In the boat!—Jesus!"

"But even without the actual words," said Ames, "I should have de-duced the truth from the testimony of the telephone girl. She remembered that Handsome Creek had been 'hard to get.' That meant, didn't it, that she had rung Handsome Creek at least twice? Yet no doubt you'll recall Isham's account: that he was right beside the telephone when it rang, and answered it at once. Therefore, the second ring meant simply a second connection. A second call put in for the same number, answered directly from the library and not heard by Isham because he had the vacuum cleaner running."

Hoopes nodded again. He was crushed.

"The girl at the switchboard was in the midst of a feminine spat. The second call meant nothing to her except that the first one hadn't been answered. And to Allison, overhearing from the next booth, the words 'I didn't tell you' seemed to refer back to a conversation held when Voorhees left the river, not to a conversation finished but a minute ago.—All the confusions, you see, were mental. The facts were simple. Voorhees talked to the same person twice."

"And I," said the low, grating voice, "had been blessing my stars for a close shave!"

I thought of the sensations of the man who had answered both those calls, as he sat listening with the sheriff and the rest of us, to Allison's story. I remembered his forehead pearled with sweat. "Those ten minutes in the dining-room," he said to Ames, "made me think I had a charmed life. Well—what next?"

"I realized that Voorhees must have made some discovery at the river. It made him denounce you, though not yet publicly; it made him refuse to break your bread, and decide to leave your roof. Already I had a dim idea of what it must be, and I could see it as sufficiently important to lead to murder, if that offered you a hope of permanent safety.

"Next, in Gertrude's and Carter's account, came the sequence of events after dinner. I was able to satisfy myself that the whole card-playing expedition to Elmington was your idea. I noted that it removed from the scene those three restless and energetic members of the house-party, particularly Freddy, who might otherwise have thought of something to take them into the library. You were risking no premature discoveries there! Nor were you taking the chance of some genial impulse on Freddy's part to help you welcome Voorhees at the door. With Gertrude and the young people eliminated, Miss Perryman barricaded behind a backgammon-table, and Carter immobilized with a book, you could pull off your plan to meet Voorhees alone. Had your very uncommon mind worked rapidly enough, at the telephone, to think of suggesting to him the west door?"

"It was obvious that my best chance was to get him to come in by the door that was farthest away," was the composed reply. "I didn't want anything he might say to be heard."

"May I ask what he did say?"

"He said, 'Let's have our show-down at once.' And I had already planned what to answer—in a loud voice, of course, words that wouldn't sound suspicious to him, and yet would mislead the others."

Ames nodded. "You said, 'Why, of course! There are pens and paper in the library. Come in'—or something like that. And it worked perfectly."

"But I am humiliated to confess that I did not think of the west door till after he had rung off, the first time. Luckily for my plans, he called up twice."

"No wonder you have felt you bore a charmed life.—Next, I came to the apparently insuperable difficulty about the radio. I *knew* that it must have been manipulated in some way after Voorhees' death to provide you with an alibi, but I could think of no explanation except a confederate. Old Isham was, to my mind, definitely out. I thought, however, of Georgia. I even thought of Mrs. Moreland! And then the electrician gave me the clue: there was a fuse-box in the cupboard! You had moved the extra games to that new place before dinner; you were able then to turn the radio—and of course simultaneously the lights—off and on from there!"

"You got a break," commented the voice.

"I hope I should have been able to work it out eventually, even without that. Perhaps by thinking about that discourse on hogs. You had been doing something with the radio before dinnertime; of course you were really tuning in on the station you meant to use after you had disposed of Voorhees, you were getting everything just right before you cut off the current at the box. And when you started to mention to the family what you had been listening to, you suddenly realized you didn't want to name that station. The only other number you could recall was, of course, from the nine o'clock list you had studied when you were picking out something to play over Voorhees' dead body. You never expected to be checked up. Am I right?"

"You know damn well you're right."

"But the electrician saved me a tot of time and hard thinking. And when I sat listening to Gertrude, that first night, I still had a long way to go.—It seemed clear that you had expected the body to be discovered by Paul. With whatever consequences to himself our suspicions might suggest. But as time passed and passed, and Paul wasn't heard from, you had to revise your scheme. The body must now be discovered by Carter, nobody else was eligible. You could not throw suspicion on him, of course, but it was too late to worry about that; you must find a pretext for sending him into the other room. So you slipped the cards off of the card-table, while

Miss Perryman was talking to Georgia, and found for them a perfectly in-spired hiding-place—the kind that would not seem to be one, but merely the thoughtless choice of a tall person like Isham, who did not reflect that he was making them invisible to anyone below his own height. Neither Miss Perryman nor Carty could see into that blue bowl, but I realized that you yourself easily could; and I remembered Carty's telling how you had played with the mantel ornaments. Still, your trick was a remarkable bit of ingenuity in a pinch. Unfortunately, the original search for the cards made it possible for Miss Perryman to beat Carter to the discovery of the crime. You shouldn't have let her get on her feet."

Cousin Lydia's illegitimate great-nephew scowled, but this time it was at himself. "I wouldn't have had that happen for worlds," he said sincerely.

"With the course of events so plain, therefore, up to the enigma of the radio," continued Ames, "I still found myself for a while quite baffled by that. And even after that riddle was solved, there remained the bare chance that Voorhees had been mistaken at the river. He hadn't actually got your shirt off your back. Of course, if he was mistaken, then you had no motive to commit murder. I must look for somebody else.—At which point I learned that the one person who had seen you stripped, old Isham, manifestly as honest a human being as I ever laid eyes on, said that the scar was there!"

"That had me stumped myself, for a few minutes."

Ames said: "You have, of course, extraordinary nerves. Most men's minds, after the shock of hearing they had been spied upon in those cir-cumstances, would have been without power to function. Yet right there (having the advantage of knowing that Isham's statement was wholly false, and yet plainly seeing that he didn't dream he was lying) you outguessed me. You divined the truth: Isham was describing something he had really and truly seen—once upon a time. But not at the time he had claimed. To make sure, you thought of a test. You made him count those coins. And watched how he did it."

At this point I think we all felt as if we were hearing a conversation in an unknown tongue. Only Ames and his partner in this extraordinary dialogue understood each other.

"And so I realized Freddy's danger," Ames continued, "when it became clear that he had almost uncovered Isham's secret. If I had been present, that evening, he would never have been allowed to leave the house alone. Someone ought to have prevented him, anyway.—But your technique of

agitating the minds of your family and guests till they simply forgot to reason, was brilliant! Your tactics—the introduction of those distracting top-
ics: the threatened operation and the new will; the daring loan of the pistol—they were extraordinary! And the very short time you gave yourself!"

The almost indifferent answer was: "I'm a good runner. I could have
got to the quarry and back even faster."

"But, professor!" I broke in, almost panting, for I was by this time miles
behind, "what was Isham's secret?"

"A most pathetic one. Just that he was going blind! Georgia knew, but
nobody else. And Freddy had seen him practicing to be ready for the total
darkness, poor old soul."

I suppose there was a deepened horror in the eyes that we turned on
Isham's slayer then, for Ames addressed him quickly, almost compassionately: "You only meant him to be injured, not killed, I believe? Laid up till
I had gone home?" Our prisoner nodded. "So, when the family had gone
downstairs and before the maids came up, you got the wardrobe door arranged, the door with the mirror in it; and at the end made him turn up the
light overhead. He could see the reflected light then, he could dimly see his
own figure against it, and he believed the mirror still to be parallel with the
wall. It steered him far enough out of his way to send him pitching down
the stairs."

"Nobody else on earth," was the somber answer, "would have guessed
that! Why, I worked harder to keep Isham's secret, after I guessed it, than
he did himself. I planned errands for him that would seem to require the
use of eyesight. I even sent him for a special book—by name!"

"Yes, but it was the very end book on a certain shelf, and of course you
told him that. I looked, I saw its position, where even a totally blind man
could have found it. You made ingenious use of his blindness, too, when
you sent him into a room from which the electric current was cut off, to
fetch a paper. You told him exactly where to lay his hands on it; you knew he
wouldn't even try to turn on the lights. He was the one person in the house to
whom lights meant nothing. But everybody else would have been willing to
swear the circuit was in perfect order after dinner, because Isham had gone
in there to look for a newspaper, and found it.—And of course for your own
lethal purposes, later on, light enough would come in from the hall!"

"And *that's* why," Allison exclaimed, "he made Ann Page call Elmington in the dark! And when the number was busy, gave her the veterinary's

number to call for him, quick, so that she wouldn't need to look in the book! He was keeping her from finding out that the library light wouldn't work.—But here's my special puzzle: what was the whirring noise, when Isham was killed?"

"Shall I tell him?" asked Ames of my new cousin.

"Do you know that too?"

"Wasn't it the window-shade?" The other nodded. "You see," said Ames to us all, "the end window, facing the stairs, was particularly bright with moonlight. Isham could have dimly got his position by that. Steered by that. Maybe missed a fall. So the shade had to be pulled down. And a person running by could easily give it a twitch and let it go snapping up to the top as he passed. If Lena had noticed the shade, or anyone had identified the sound, the action wasn't suspicious in itself. More light was welcome. And as it happened, nobody spotted it."

"Except you."

"Just by simplifying again," said Ames. "All the others were racking their brains for a thoroughly sinister explanation of the sound. Otherwise they'd have identified that harmless, familiar noise as quickly as I did. Anyway, by that time I knew whose hand to look for, every time."

"And so my flight of fancy about the meal of apple pie in that abominable kitchen was thrown away?"

"Quite. But what a magnificent yarn! I suppose you thought I was too much interested in that old scoundrel Sloap, eh, and needed some dust in my eyes?"

"And don't you go thinking I enjoyed spinning the sort of yarn that would have been true of *him*—the other one! I've honestly loathed one thing about this game: that I'd borrowed the skin of a coward and a sneak. For he was a whiner and a sneak to the bone, and born that way; don't blame the bull for it! Boys know one another.—And so I've bragged like a cur about my own perfectly genuine pluck. A borrowed inferiority complex. Damn queer."

"Yes, your pluck's genuine," conceded little Ames. "And so was the dazzling originality of one thing about your campaign. You took brilliant advantage of the fact that the most effective deceptions are not addressed to the eye."

I asked, "What are they addressed to, then?" I knew I sounded stupid and petulant, but I was not yet over the shock of seeing a man turn into another man before my eyes; and Ames and our vanquished enemy seemed to me to be still conversing in a sort of code, a psychological shorthand. I repeated, "What *are* they addressed to?"

"To the other senses, naturally. Sight is so important to us that we involuntarily translate all sorts of other sense-impressions into visual terms. The ruse that made you think Voorhees a living man half an hour after he was dead in his chair was addressed altogether to the ear. Your own imaginations supplied a visual image of Voorhees alive and moving about in the library, adjusting the radio!—Then again, didn't you mentally visualize Moreland, here, walking up the front stairs? Yet, when you analyze the sources of that impression, you find just two things: cigarette smoke and a sound of jingling keys. A smell-picture and a sound-picture. That was what old dim-eyed Isham had and passed on to you. And you identified it as a description of Moreland. Whereas it was a totally different person, Isham's own familiar employer, in fact, who went up those stairs safely disguised in a smell and a sound!"

"Now I did see! To make us suspect the doctor! And when Freddy was attacked on the cliff—"

"Cigar-smoke, that time. And a cigar left on the ground to prove it."

Hoopes was breathing heavily, and mopping his brow, wet with the dews of mental effort. Ames went on.

"And the sore-throat-and-eucalyptus combination took care of the tobacco-breath afterwards, in both cases. Just as the toothbrushing-and-mouth-wash combination had taken care of the whiskey-breath after Ann Page got her fright."

"I was wondering," said the grating voice, "if you had forgotten that— that— What was it you called it while you were leading me along, and making me believe I was as safe as a church?—You called it an attempt to shake the morale of the household."

"I hadn't forgotten it. That incident had me worried for a while. It was clearly impulsive. Not planned in advance. And therefore in this case the whiskey wasn't premeditatedly taken in order to mislead. Finally I worked it out (simplifying again), that seeing Ann Page there, you simply seized a chance that happened to come up when by accident you had made yourself safe. Ergo, you had taken a drink that night in desperation, just because you *needed* a drink!"

"God! did I need it that night!"

"Just so. No doubt you took a stiff one after we came up to bed.—Then, when you had scared Ann Page, you followed her at a safe distance, got upstairs, and after a mouth-wash, the ruffian vanished." Ames smiled grimly. "I restrained Carty till you had had time to get into your room."

"You played me like a fish. What were you waiting for?"

"For you to make a mistake. If I had had more time, I think you could have been goaded into imprudence. By experimenting, I had found the means. I had learned that you were sensitive about appearing at any disadvantage before the negroes."

"'Sensitive'!" The word came out with a savage laugh. "You've never been poor-white trash, in rags that hardly covered up your nakedness, and seen the comfortable sleek colored people, the well-fed house-servants, laugh at you! That's an experience! If you had had it, the suspicion that a negro might be laughing at you would be white-hot iron on your bare skin, for life!"

"So I had a means of disturbing you emotionally, you see. Of throwing your cool reason off center. All I needed was time enough for you to make a slip. Something to give yourself away. I had no proofs, you see."

"And what slip did I make?"

"None at all! So I had to rush matters. You were about to get off and have a scar manufactured! The one thing I haven't been able to guess yet is why you didn't do it before. Supposing you were willing to run the great risk, you had plenty of chance, all those years."

"But the risk was enormous. The fellow who did the job might manage to trail the patient, and I was afraid of blackmail. Still, I'd have chanced it, I think, except for one silly little reason: I wasn't sure which side it was on!"

"I never thought of that," said Ames, in a mortified tone.

"You see, when I stripped him, it was dark. I did not think to—feel. And after I came home here again, and heard all the details, and knew what had to be done, and just where, I kept on putting it off. There seemed to be lots of time."

"You were not yet thinking of—marriage."

A light burst on my brain. "So *that* was the obstacle you meant!"

"You see, don't you," inquired Ames of me, "the point of the X-ray picture? A scar can be manufactured, I credited our friend here with enough ingenuity to think of that; but I was praying Heaven he hadn't thought of the perfectly sound bone in his left arm that ought to have showed a particularly complicated old break! And he had not— And yet," said Ames to the bare-chested listener whose arms were now unfolded, and whose hands strayed nervously, "everything—even after Voorhees' discovery—might have been so different! Your outburst when you smashed the ice-cubes struck me, you know, when I heard of it, as genuine. You had found out already that you were in the wrong place. Leading the wrong life. I believe you'd have gathered together what money was honestly yours, and disappeared again—if you hadn't fallen in love."

The mighty naked chest rose and fell as a painful breath heaved it. This man's life had been a lonely privacy of body and soul, and now both were being violated. Ames went on, "And you were ready then to move heaven and earth to remain at Handsome Creek."

The retort that came was oblique. "Voorhees was a self-righteous prig," said Jefferson Sloap hotly. "Was it my fault that old Adrian Dunn left me his money? I didn't ask for it. He left his money to me because I was the ablest Dunn in sight, and he knew it! And then comes Voorhees, threatening to expose me—" The great chest rose and fell again, the straying hands fumbled behind him. "Well—"

The room was very still. Little Ames, rumpling his white crest with an air of painful suspense, was staring with deliberate intention at the floor

There was a clink of glass from the shelves. Ames stiffened, but nobody moved. Suddenly my cousin heaved a second big breath; he was looking at the door. In the silence, a distant unmistakably happy masculine chuckle was heard, mingled with soft sounds of another voice; footsteps, the unhurried footsteps of two persons, were drawing nearer, by the river path. I thought, "No wonder Freddy's late. She has accepted him—"

Our captive straightened to his full height. His eyes flashed. He roared out a deep-chested call: "Hi! *Freddy!*"

"*Coming!*"

It all happened in a flash. The shout, as if for help, in the familiar voice, and the instant eager response. The bounding footsteps—nearer, nearer—racing footsteps of happy Freddy, answering the call of his friend.

For not preventing what happened next, I was equally to blame with Ames. Seeing that desperate hand groping towards the cyanide bottle, I had said to myself, quite correctly, "Ames is willing to let him have it." And

God knows I was willing. What we both forgot was that the cyanide wasn't the only bottle on those shelves. Beside, Ames had a pistol—

The pistol snapped harmlessly. A jeering voice said, "You didn't think I left that thing in your room with the cartridges in it, did you?" The figure at the shelves was wheeling now, a glass bottle in its hand. Yellow liquid, maybe a pint.

The next few seconds were over like lightning, yet the suspense of them seemed to last a year. I heard Ames' instinctive cry, "Catch, Robinson!" and then, as if in agony, "No! *let me!*" The white-haired old figure leaped—it was struggling to shove Robinson away from in front of the door, its face was contorted with horror. Robinson broke the clinch, struck one giant blow—no time to be gentle!—and the professor went down. He fell sitting, his terrified look never left Robinson's face, his parted lips seemed to pray!—Now, in the same instant it seemed, the furious naked arm that was swinging the bottle of vitriol hurled it with terrific force at the wall just over the door—the door in which now Freddy's tall head was suddenly seen, over Robinson's shoulder. True as a bomb, deadlier than a bomb, the bottle flew straight for the wall above their heads, and the great brown hand of Robinson—too close against the wall, great God, much too close!—shot up to stop that flying death!

The wicked whirling missile smashed into his palm. Sped with demoniac power to shatter and break and spray its liquid fire abroad, the bottle was but checked, not stopped, by Robinson's hand; the impact jerked his raised arm backward, the knuckles struck the wall with a mighty crack— and my heart stood still. It seemed impossible that anything made of glass, flung with such force, should not break when it hit, even with Robinson's fingers between it and the wood. My whole frame cringed with the horrid fear of seeing that blazing death set free—to stream down, to burn scalp from bone, and bone from brain, and make of the great-hearted negro a screaming animal before our eyes—and Freddy—Freddy— But the bottle held! Even so, every drop of blood seemed to have drained from Robinson's dark face; without an idea of what the thing contained, he had caught the terror and anguish of Ames' look—his own agate eyes fairly protruded, his skin was gray. He stood frozen now, one arm aloft, like a half-crucified man, till the professor tottered to him, and dragged his hand down, almost sobbing, "You blessed damn fool, Robinson, give that thing to me!"

To this day Ames doesn't like to talk about the moment when, thanks to his purely instinctive order and Robinson's automatic response, Robinson's life hung by a hair. Nor would the good fellow's death have saved Freddy. In fact, all of us would have come in for some drops of that hell. Therefore, when we had time to look again at Jefferson Sloap, and saw him fallen twitching to the floor, the cyanide's business this time authentically done, Moreland spoke for us all when he said solemnly, "Thank God!"

I quavered, "But merciful Heavens!—did he simply go mad at the end?"

Ames took the bottle from Robinson with shaking hands. "You might call it that. And—God forgive me for what almost happened—I wasn't prepared! And yet I had seen through his pose, his strenuous pretending that the obstacle to his taking a wife was the one that's obvious when the beloved is a married woman. But the real obstacle, the insuperable one, to his marrying anybody he wanted to, was that he didn't have the famous scar. When he made up his mind to the risks of having a surgical imitation made—no more waiting!—I knew that he was desperate. I should have been ready."

"Ready for t-t-this?" I pointed at the bottle like a child, I was shaking worse than he.

"For some supreme explosion of his awful devouring jealousy of Freddy! And his hopeless passion for— Hush!"

Ann Page stood in the door.

The suicide of Voorhees' host was accepted by everyone as a tacit explanation of the death of Voorhees; the whole inquiry dropped. As for Isham, he needed no avenging now, we felt; he slept well. And justice had been served.

Human nature is strangely mixed. What is man, that he should judge his fellow? My cousin's will, we found, left all—our great-grandfather's house, his uncle's money, the family treasures, everything—to "Miss Lydia Perryman, my kind and dearly-loved friend, that she may by her own will and testament equitably distribute them." Cousin Lydia's agitated tears dripped suddenly on the page that did not call her "my aunt." And my own throat had a lump in it.

COACHWHIP PUBLICATIONS
COACHWHIPBOOKS.COM

THE COUNSELLOR

J. J. CONNINGTON

THE FOUR DEFENCES

J. J. CONNINGTON

COACHWHIP PUBLICATIONS
COACHWHIPBOOKS.COM

COACHWHIP PUBLICATIONS
COACHWHIPBOOKS.COM

ANITA BOUTELL

DEATH BRINGS
A STORKE

CRADLED
IN FEAR

MURDER

IN A WALLED TOWN

KATHERINE WOODS

COACHWHIP PUBLICATIONS
COACHWHIPBOOKS.COM

THE CAT
SCREAMS
A HUGH RENNERT MYSTERY

TODD DOWNING

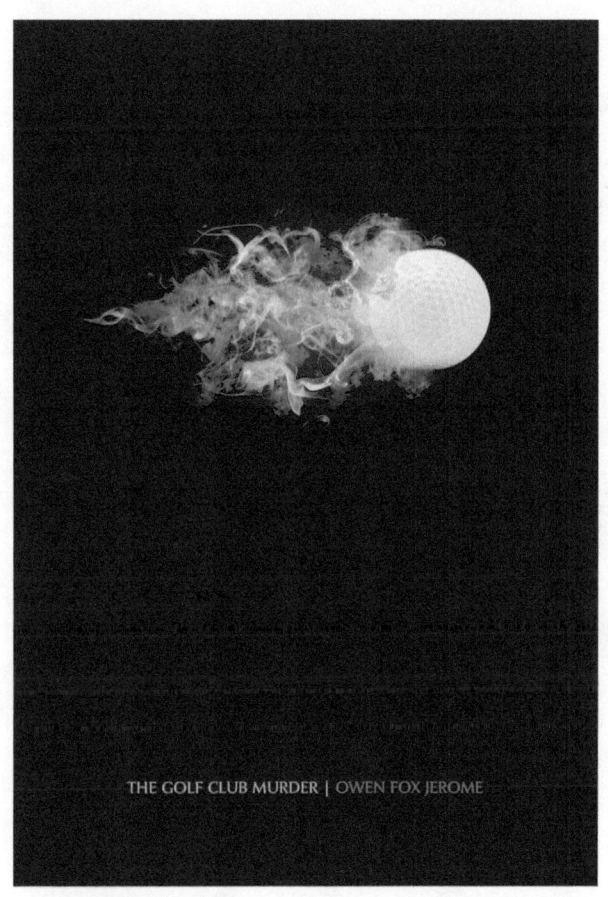

www.ingramcontent.com/pod-product-compliance
Lightning Source LLC
Chambersburg PA
CBHW020640250626
47154CB00008B/2755